No-Injury Policy

Short Fiction By

C.M. HUMPHRIES

This is a work of fiction. Names, characters, corporations, institutions, organizations, events or locales in this story collection are either the product of the author's imaginations or, if real, used fictitiously. Any resemblance to actual persons (living or dead) is entirely coincidental.

NO-INJURY POLICY
a Chase County Book
CHASE COUNTY PUBLISHING

Paperback edition published 2012.
New Matte Paperback edition published 2013.

For information address: C.M. Humphries
ISBN-13: 978-0615719733 (C.M. Humphries)
ISBN-10: 0615719732

No-Injury Policy

Table of Contents

To Rosalie, who figured if you had a pen and a name, you could write a book. As it turns out, she was right.

All Things Beautiful

I.

They shoved the boy in his bedroom and locked the door.

At eleven years old, the boy was still skittish when it came to being alone, and even more timid when it came to dealing with other people. Outside of the room, he'd play with his sister Joan in the vast hallways, ones so eloquently decorated they might've belonged to an art museum.

In fact, the entire house might've contained more paintings than any art galleria in Chase County, but the boy had only been to one, when he was nine. Like most activities in his life, the visits to museums, amusement parks, and zoos only occurred once or twice. Even his family trips to the library were short-lived, although the boy learned to read at an accelerated rate according to the librarians.

His parents, though possessing the accumulative self-depth of a ghost at times, used to be so proud of him—their little Devon. Soon, they stopped spending time with him and stopped addressing him by anything other than, "Damn it, boy!"

Only one person still spent time with him: His sister Joan. So when his parents were away or at work, and when the butler was preoccupied, Devon played with his sister in the upstairs hallways.

The game started off as hide n' seek and ended in

a chase. "I found you," Joan would say. "You're so ugly I could spot you in a swamp!"

It was inevitable that their heavy steps would call the attention of their parents or the butler. That's when their playtime ended.

On the last day Devon and Joan played, they swore not to chase and to be quiet. A brittle silence raised the hairs on Devon's arms when he noticed his sister was already hushed. Almost against herself, she said, "All right. I'll count and you go hide first."

Devon, having hidden in every other room on the third floor, decided to try something new. He cracked open his bedroom door only enough to slide in and thumb it shut.

Despite the gentle *click* of the lock, Devon felt safe in the company of silence. He glanced around at his room.

One corner of the wall was laced with a small library, since his parents now prohibited further library visits. Another wall shared space with a small closet, which held very few articles of clothing on the hangers. The wall across from the closet was home to an antiquated armoire lined with a snowdrift of dust that served as a wintery domicile for random stationary.

Devon stared at his twin bed next. It was nothing more than a car-shaped frame with a broken backboard, but he never found anything except comfort from it. He slid underneath the bed, where dust bunnies cluttered in fear, and he waited to be found.

Although being a good hider was an award of the game, being found was fulfilling. It meant someone searched for you. It meant you were wanted.

And he waited for such satisfaction. No footsteps echoed across the hallways. No small shadows slipped under the door. He'd won.

After what felt like an eternity of waiting, Devon scooted out from underneath the bed and tiptoed for the door. He contemplated turning the handle, when suddenly, he heard footsteps outside. He crouched down and fought a snicker as he listened. A shadow swayed in the light seeping through the cracks of the door. Before long, there were multiple shapes. His parents were searching for him too! Then, he had the perfect idea: He would pop out of the room and scare them.

Devon rushed to his feet and reached for the handle, but before he could perform his little scare, it turned on its own and *clicked*.

One look at the doorknob and Devon knew something was wrong. Someone had faced the lock towards the hallway so it couldn't be unlocked from the inside. He fidgeted with the door and screamed out, "Hey, I'm locked in! This isn't funny, Joanie. Let me out!"

A few minutes passed and Devon knew he was stuck. "Mom? Dad?" he tried to yell, but his voice was too hoarse.

The boy flopped to the ground and placed his head between his knees. He wished he could've cried, but his parents prohibited such behavior.

II.

Even without a clock in the room, the boy knew hours had passed, and judging by the way his stomach churned, it was near lunchtime.

Over the growl of his stomach, the boy heard the roar of an engine. He stood up and rushed over to the window. A *crack* followed the impact of his knees on the mattress as he propped himself up to stare out at the front yard.

A SUV backed along the forested driveway below and headed down to the crossing highway. In the front seats, his parents looked up only once at his bedroom before they resisted eye contact. His sister, however, pressed her face against the side window and stared the boy's face with swollen eyes until the SUV was out of sight.

The boy kept watching even though his family was gone. In the same manner some people waited next to their mailboxes, the boy kept observing the driveway, hoping his family would return.

After another hour or so, he sunk down on his bed and placed his head back between his knees. As silence began to sweep over the room, there came a faint tintinnabulation from the door.

Like a phantom, the butler snuck into the room as though he'd walked right through the wall. By the light peeking in from outside, the boy distinguished a silver platter in the butler's hands. It was bedazzling, the platter, with detailed silver flowers carved around the edges. Atop of the mirror center was a sandwich and a glass of water.

The butler placed the platter on top of the dresser and pivoted for the door. On his way out, the boy asked him, "When are they coming back?"

With glass-like tears frozen at the corner of his eyes, the butler wrinkled his lips but said nothing before he turned away and locked the door shut behind him.

The boy quivered but did not cry. Instead, he stumbled towards the dresser and ate this meal on the floor, across from the bed. At the last bite of his sandwich, the boy gulped down the water until he saw a smudge at the halfway point. Upon closer examination, he realized it wasn't a smudge at all. He saw something through the bottom of the glass. Something protruded from the frame of the bed.

He crawled away from the crumb-covered platter and reached for a loose spring underneath the bed. As it broke away, the edge of the spring sliced his fingertip.

While he sucked the blood away from the cut, the boy toyed with the spring until it was straight. With the straightened spring in hand, he headed for the door.

On his side of the doorknob was a small hole. He remembered how his parents replaced all the locks with this type in case they ever needed to break in. Before Joan was born, the boy threw a conniption and locked himself inside the bedroom. His father found a way in by using a Q-tip with a broken off cotton swab.

Likewise, the boy slid the straightened spring into the small hole and felt for the lock.

A scrape of metal against metal sent chills through the boy's arms like the aluminum tip of a pencil scraping along a desk. He dropped the spring and shook off the shivers, but he knew all he had to do now was press in the lock.

He placed the edge of the spring back into the lock and felt around. The metal connected! The boy jumped to his feet and pressed in, when the spring snapped and fell inside the doorknob. Confusion consumed his face as he stared at the lock in disbelief. Even if he discovered another loose piece of metal, the lock was jammed.

The boy ambled through the darkened room and flicked on a lamp near his bed. His eyes darted over to his small library. At the very least, he could've passed the time until his family returned home. Soon enough they'd realize they'd forgotten him, wouldn't they?

III.

His lunch arrived early the next day.

Halfway through Mary Shelley's *Frankenstein; or, the Modern Prometheus*, the boy placed the book to the side and sprinted towards the door in an attempt to sneak out of the room before the butler locked it shut. The plan failed.

The boy walked over to the platter and snatched his lunch. Today it was macaroni and cheese. There were times when he felt the butler was just emptying out the pantry. He ate his meal one slow bite at a time.

Eating became quite a chore after his meals became quick cooks, such as the sandwiches and pasta variations. They always came around the same times too—save this particular meal—and he only ate at lunch and dinnertime. Breakfast must've required too much preparation from the butler, or his parents forgot to shop before they took off. When he finished forcing down his meal, the boy left the plate on the floor and returned to his bed, where he continued gazing out of the window on a sinking hope for his family's return.

A van pulled into the drive. It certainly wasn't the SUV his folks left in, but he was excited nonetheless. Soon enough, he heard footsteps thumping in the foyer two stories below. While his family all had hard steps, he could never hear them from the third floor in such clarity. Maybe it was his folks; maybe it wasn't. Either way, someone could help him out of the room.

As he rushed to the door, it slammed open, the hard wood frame slapping him across the face. No sooner than he regained his balance, the butler bent down and taped a piece of cloth across his mouth. Hesitant at first, the butler grabbed the silver platter and smacked the boy across the head, rendering him unconscious.

∞

When he awoke, the boy heard the van's engine start. He tried to scream as the visitors backed down the driveway, but the cloth was sealed tight around his lips. As he pulled the tape and cloth off with one hand, the boy pounded against the window, but the van was gone by then.

He sat down and stared at the cloth and the dented silver platter. And idea struck. He brought the plate near the window and angled it until a concentrated beam of light bounced onto the floor. He scooted the cloth in front of the beam's end and waited until it began to burn. The boy discovered fire. He already knew much of flames, but he created these on his own, without a lighter. With a free foot, he stomped out the cloth and grinned. Fire was ubiquitous, but creating his own was something truly satisfying.

IV.

Eleven sunsets passed and the boy's meals were becoming a juxtaposition of various garnishes and snack foods. It didn't matter to him after the fourth sunset; for he'd lost his appetite and let the platters build up in the corner one by one.

Why the butler stopped picking up the leftovers eluded the boy's mind. Perhaps, the butler noticed he wasn't eating and thought a variety of meals would tantalize his taste buds. But they didn't.

After the twelfth sunset, the butler's tears stopped flowing, and he stopped showing up altogether.

Ants barged in the room through the little cracks around the door, which inspired the boy to bring the food near the window. Just as he'd burned the cloth, the boy waited for the sun to beam into his room and then burned the army of ants as soon as they fell for the bait. Soon enough, a grey sky swallowed the sunlight, which left the food to the never ending swarm of ants.

They reminded him of *Frankenstein* and the other books he'd read. Like ants, humans would keep fighting even in the promise of death, so long as they loathed or lusted something enough. What was funny was the ants all sacrificed their lives for something the boy didn't even want.

He turned away from the ants and watched the storm as it brewed outside. The rain drew thicker, the clouds blacker, and the wind grew a tail to whip against the house. Around the van that returned earlier, a small flood began to current down the long driveway.

As the wind kissed his window, each time with more enthusiasm, a small breath chilled his arms. The boy wiped the dust from the window to see if there was a crack.

He found no sign of damage to the window, a fact which led to the boy trying to lift the window open. Sometimes the simplest solutions only came with time. To his surprise, the window slid open enough for the boy to slither onto the rooftop.

Twenty feet below the window stood a group of four men in uniform trying to puff down the last of their cigarettes under a sky that excreted like a ringed sponge. The boy remembered Frankenstein's monster and how he—no, *it*—escaped into the villages.

Literature had brought premonition to the boy. He didn't know what experience lay before him once he left the room, but something didn't feel quite right. Something about the men below struck fear into the boy. If they spoke to him, he wouldn't know what to say. He'd never known what to say to his own family.

In the whip of gyrating woes, the boy also realized this was his only chance to reunite with his family. The boy fidgeted with the window for another inch of space and crawled along the gritty and wet shingles. The men in the driveway stomped out their cigarette butts and headed for the front door, completely unaware of the boy as he struggled to remain flat on the rooftop. The boy watched until they were out of his immediate view and walked towards the lowest edge of the roof. Lightning tore the black construction paper sky into slivers, and caught off-guard by the sight, the boy misplaced his foot near the gutter. He felt the grit of the shingles scrape along his arms and neck. And then he felt nothing at all.

V.

"Jesus," a man with a smokey growl behind his voice said. "You think the kid's all right?"

"I dunno," another replied.

For a few seconds, the boy only saw a distorted slice of reality, something black with outlines of light. One at a time, his eyelids retreated. Standing tall above the boy were the four men from earlier, before the fall.

"Where are your parents?" the growly man asked.

The boy couldn't answer. He remembered it all too well and wanted to shout what happened, but how could he tell a stranger that his parents went out and forgot about him? He would cause them trouble for which he would certainly be punished.

"It's okay, little man," the growly man said. "My name's Stan. Stan Williams You can trust me."

The boy nodded.

Stan smiled and asked, "So do you know where your parents are? Did you take off from them?"

The boy didn't know.

"Where do you live?"

Underneath a sharp ray of sun unique to such a rainy day, the boy turned his head to the side and stared at his upstairs bedroom.

Stan shielded his eyes with one hand and studied the house. "Not this one," he said.

∞

Inside the house, Stan and his crew followed the boy to the dining room. There, the butler strolled towards the table with paperwork in his hands. He fought to mask a grin until he spotted the boy sitting by Stan at the front of the table. The boy followed the paperwork with his eyes as every last page swayed to the floor before they scattered apart.

"Are you all right?" Stan asked the butler. "Mister Harrington?"

The butler remained static.

"Tom," Stan said, "are you okay?"

Thomas Harrington leaned down on one knee and started scooping the papers back together in a sloppy stack. "Ah yes," he said. "Just stood up too fast or someth—a blackout while standing up."

"Umm okay, Mister Harrington. You all right to do this?"

Tom let the papers drop straight down from his hands. He wiped his head along his sports coat and said, "Ah . . . let . . . me . . . Let me that for a moment too . . . Just catch my breath. That blackout really took it out of me." And then he darted for the front door.

Stan sprinted after the butler, and soon the rest of the crew jumped up from their seats and followed suit. Once all the men pursued Tom outside, the boy walked over to the dining room windows. At the end of the driveway, Tom rushed into the highway as a truck sped up the hill. Stan came from behind and tackled the butler to the driveway. As they left sight, the rest of the crew met at the end of the driveway and started conversing with Tom. After they finished, the butler gathered the rest of his belongings and left the grounds. Meanwhile, Stan and his crew met back up in the dining room, where the boy now sat the end of the table.

Stan stood at the opposite end and said, "You start working while I drop the boy off with Susan." He glanced at the boy and said, "C'mon."

VI.

Stan and Susan lived in the smallest house the boy had ever seen. It made him recall how difficult it was to visualize the village homes in *Frankenstein*. When Stan led the boy into his house, they started off through a small living room with some sort of animal head attached to the wall above the television.

Next they entered the kitchen, which had an old stove, no artwork or pleasing aesthetic make up, and a small breakfast table as the only furniture. The three of them sat around the table—the boy sitting on a stack of milk crates, an ammunition crate, and a pillow as a makeshift chair cushion.

Susan, Stan's wife, leaned in to whisper in her husband's ear, but the boy could hear every word she said: "What about his parents?"

Stan started to whisper back: "That's the thing. The old butler said they left . . . no idea where they went or if they're . . . ." The boy couldn't hear everything Stan said the same way he understood his wife.

His wife replied, "There's no way we can take care of him. We don't know if you're gonna keep getting jobs like the one at his house."

"Then we'll . . . until his parents come into . . . or they're . . . . Either way, we'll wait . . . days and . . . ." Stan said. He stood back up and stretched. "Well," he said to both the boy and Susan, "I've gotta get back to work. You two have fun, all right?" He looked at the boy. "Why don't you tell her your name, little man?"

Stan and Susan waited for the boy to reply. When he didn't, Stan said, "Well, you two have a good day. I'll see you both later tonight." And he left.

"So," Susan said, trying to break an ongoing silence, "what do you like to do?"

The boy remained to himself.

"Now that's no way to have fun," she said. "C'mon, you can tell me. What do you like to do? Do you like to play any games?"

The boy recalled how much he used to play hide n' seek with his sister Joan. That was until he found himself locked in the bedroom.

"C'mon," Susan pleaded. "Do you want to watch some TV?"

"Devon," the boy said.

"Oh my!" Susan replied. "See how easy that was? What is that, a show or—Oh, your *name's* Devon."

Devon nodded.

"All right, *Devon*," Susan said, "What do you like to do for fun?"

"Are my parents dead?"

She froze. "What? No, of course not, honey. They just went somewhere. They'll be back. You're just—uh—gonna stay here for a bit. Until they come back."

"So they left me?" Devon asked.

"No, no, no. They just had to do something important. Do you want something to eat? Are you hungry, Devon?"

VII.

Stan returned home, as promised, but it was late. According to the television menu, it was almost eleven at night. He sat on a Laz E Boy across from the couch and asked Devon, "So I heard you got a name."

Devon stayed quiet and stared at the TV.

"Well—uh—Where's Susan?"

Devon pointed to the back hallway by nodding.

"Oh, she's asleep. I think I'm gonna join her. It's been a long day. If you want you can set a sleep timer . . ." Stan walked over and snatched the remote control.

A screen prompted a time option when he pressed a button near the bottom. He handed the controller over to Devon and said, "Select whatever time you think you'll fall asleep. Goodnight, Devon."

He headed down the hallway, and Devon grinned as he watched TV until his eyes drew heavy.

∞

Devon awoke to the sound of the front door slamming against the coat closet's. Through peered eyelids, he scoped out the entrance and saw a young man—maybe in his upper-teens—stumble into the home and looked directly into his bloodshot eyes. The young man stared back at him.

"What the hell are you doing in my house?" he asked with slurred words. "Who the hell are you?"

Devon didn't know how to respond to the enraged young man. He wasn't like the rest of them. He didn't ask again, and he didn't wait for an answer. Instead, the young man rushed towards the TV and kicked straight through the screen. As he pulled back and fumbled to the floor, Devon chuckled for a brief second until he realized what he might've done. He might've provoked the belligerent young man.

"What the hell's so funny, punk?" the young man asked with clenched teeth.

Seething as he ran forward, the young man soon charged into Devon until they both crashed through the small coffee table. Devon struggled to catch his wind and grasped his chest. At the sound of chaos,

Stan hurried down the hall with heavy steps and stood at the living room entrance.

"What's going on?" he asked. He took one look at Devon and added, "This is Devon, Gary, and he's gonna stay here for awhile. I'm not asking you to accept him as a brother, but please treat him like one for now."

VIII.

For the first two weeks, Gary was the kindest person Devon had met. Not even Joan was so caring. He would help Devon make lunch and find *Frankenstein* movies and cartoons—almost none of which came close to depicting the story as Devon imagined it. But by week three, Gary and Devon held to different views of "like family."

Down a side hall, in Gary's room, Devon was in a corner weeping. All around him was darkness. Black walls with red corners. Posters with names he'd never heard. Gary played distorted music at the peak of his large stereo's capacity, and Devon cringed every time Gary waved the copy of *Frankenstein.*

"You're an idiot," Gary said. "There's no way you could read this. You're too dumb. *I* can't even read this."

Devon continued crying and begging for his book.

Gary raised the book over a few candles and let the flames chew at the edges. "You still want it?"

Devon stopped quivering and sprung to his feet in a scramble to steal back the book. Surprised by the rush, Gary lost his grip on the book.

"You little fucker," Gary said. He picked up the largest candle and turned it upside down on Devon.

At first, the wax burned deep. Within a matter of seconds, the pain faded away, although Devon couldn't shake off the gut-wrenching fear of the moment. The boy felt worse than alone; he felt at war with all other human beings.

VIV.

Months or years flew by—the boy didn't really know. The days were all blurred by the constant puzzling turn of events. On this day, the boy walked down to the garage, where he hoped to find Stan with or without Gary. He didn't want to encounter the young man alone. In the garage, a cool stale air brushed by, bringing scents the boy had never encountered. He recognized one of the aromas: fuel.

In spite of the stinging smells looming in the darkened garage, the boy approached the center, admittedly, with crippling trepidation. He heard feet scuffle before a load roar filled the garage. The boy winced at the sound, but soon sunlight greeted him.

"You ready to go fishing?" Stan said as Gary stepped out from the boat in the corner of the garage.

The boy nodded and only stopped when Gary glared at him with a warped beam.

∞

A brisk drizzle filled most of the morning, but the weather couldn't stop their fishing trip. There were channels at the end of the lake so vast and dark they needed to use flashlights. The boy never experienced such a sight when he saw the light reflecting off of the fish scales down below. The water remained in blackness while a small radius within the beam was ever so clear. As his excitement grew, the boy remembered the way Gary looked at him before the ride to the lake.

The image of his razor grin chilled the boy. He felt something ominous was bound to happen, so he started to squirm in place and look at Stan.

"Do you have to pee?" Stan asked.

The boy nodded.

Stan steered the boat to a peninsula shore. He dropped down the anchor, which was nothing more than an old boat motor welded to a chain. "Just go behind one of those trees," Stan said.

The boy wasn't quite sure of his whereabouts, but he possessed the inclination he could find his way home from the woods. As soon as the boy touched the edge of the peninsula, he heard Stan say, "Gary, you might as well go now. I know you'll ask later."

The boy stopped heading for the woods.

"What's a matter, Devon? Don't you have to go?" Stan asked.

Although the boy needed to go in the worst way, he shook his head.

"I thought you just said—C'mon, boy. Don't be scared. It's part of being a man."

Gary reached the top hill of the peninsula by the time Stan gestured for the boy to move, and the boy did so.

When the boy approached the forested depths a little beyond the hill, he didn't see Gary. He could hear him *going*, but he drifted off somewhere out of sight. This was the boy's window. The boy darted into the woods, following an unkempt trail. He didn't know where he headed; nonetheless, it was away from Gary.

That was until he heard, "Where do you think you're going, dumbass?"

Without one look back, the boy sprinted until his knees felt like spheres of splinters. His sides cramped and daggered every last nerve. Ignoring the pain, he rushed to the end of the woods, where he stumbled before the edge of a steep cliff.

A few feet away from the edge, the boy turned towards the woods and awaited Gary. Small streams ran though the mud and inched towards the cliff with every second.

The boy turned towards the far west side of the woods and yelled, "Where are you?"

After those three words, he resumed his command over silence. But soon the silence was severed by soft steps behind him. The boy pivoted around to fall into the tight grasp of Gary's hands on his shoulder, thumbs nearing both major pressure points.

Gary said, "What are you doing? God, you're so fucking hideous. Where the hell did you come from?" Still latched on the boy's shoulders, Gary started to shove him forward, closer and closer to the edge. "You know, no one's gonna miss you. They'll just pretend like it never happened."

As Gary pushed the boy forward, his leg became trapped by the boy's. The boy tackled Gary down, one slow shove at a time, but near the edge.

Something rushed over the boy. Rather than burst with anger, he fell into confusion, which made him want to send Gary off the edge of the cliff even more.

"What's taking you boys so long up here?" Stan said upon his emergence from the blackened woods. "Jesus Christ, boy, what the hell are you doing to my son?"

X.

The house reeked of quiet for ten days—maybe fifteen or two months— it didn't matter. Soon enough, Gary convinced everyone it was the boy who was a liability no one could ever afford.

A small bus came to the end of the cul-de-sac and stopped in front of the house. Although Stan, Susan, and Gary all waited at the door and waved him on, they never said goodbye. No one said they were going to miss him except Gary.

Onto the bus, the boy walked past three rows of empty seats before stopping. He stood in awe at the emergency exit.

"Come along, little man," the driver, a redheaded woman around her mid-thirties, said. "What's your name?"

The boy didn't say a word.

"Well, why don't you find a seat?"

The boy walked to the end of the bus. He leaned against the side of a stiff seat to watch the world drift behind him.

"Face the front please," the driver said.

He did.

The driver started driving faster as she looked in the rearview mirror with a somewhat sincere smile and said, "Thank you, *Devon*, There's a seat belt if you need it."

∞

Devon reached the end of the bus steps before the driver opened the doors. With one last smile, the driver pulled the door lever and revealed a playground full of kids of different ages. Beyond the playground stood a large building with dozens of small windows. Once the bus drove away, an elderly woman approached Devon and tapped on his shoulder.

Devon shuddered and turned to face her.

"Didn't mean to startle you," the woman said. "I'm Cindy and this is my home. Come with me, won't you Devon?" She reached out for Devon to grab her hand.

Hand-in-hand, Cindy led Devon through the gate of the playground, walking past damaged jungle gyms, seesaws and swing sets for the younger children, and a basketball court and set of benches for the older children. Though the outdoor area was immaculate and maintained, it was a little darker where two of the older children hung out. In the shade of the building's corners, two kids a few years older than Devon hid to smoke cigarettes.

Cindy saw Devon's focus turn to the chain-smokers, and she tried to deter his attention. "I'll let you explore out here later, but let me show you around inside."

Following a few feet behind, Devon walked with Cindy into the house. Overheard, an antiquated chandelier dangled from an old silver-plated chain, and plastic trees decorated the areas around two or three office doors. To the right of a staircase in the center, a mix of children (mostly near his age) sat around a television set in an enormous living room that resembled more of a game room with an old TV set, tarnished furniture, and a weathered pool table.

"That over there is our living quarters," Cindy said. "Whenever you have free time, you'll be able to hang out with the other children."

She started to walk towards a staircase, and Devon followed. Upstairs wasn't decorated like the first floor. All the beige paint on the walls appeared new from afar, but as Cindy led him further along the upstairs hallway, Devon noticed all the patched holes and faint stains beneath the top coat.

There were thirteen rooms in all. Devon's was lucky number thirteen, a somewhat larger room at the very end of the hallway. The closer they got to the room, the more Devon could smell cigarette smoke.

Cindy stepped further ahead of Devon and knocked on the door, despite how she jiggled the doorknob seconds later. A thunderous roll of footsteps traveled from each side of the room to the other—Devon could feel it through vibrations underfoot. The shuffle ceased and the handle *clicked* until a boy's face appeared between the door and its frame. He was the boy smoking with a same-aged girl outside. "Yes, Miss Cindy?" he asked.

Cindy stiff-armed the door open and plowed into the room. A violent waft of stale smoke poured out, but she ignored it. As Devon snuck into the room behind Cindy, they both turned to face the boy and his female counterpart.

"Now Zach and Karen," Cindy said, "I want you to meet Devon. This is his first day here, and I'd appreciate it if you could make him feel at home." She turned to speak with Devon. "Zachary here is your roommate. It's been awhile since he's had someone to share a room with, so I'm sure he's excited to finally have a buddy."

"Absolutely stoked," Zach said plainly, to which, Karen was forced to muffle a laugh.

"Before I leave you three to yourselves, Zach, can I see you in the hall for a minute?"

Zach followed Cindy out. Door closed behind them, they started to converse. Devon heard some of what was said:

"What did I tell you about smoking inside?" Cindy asked. "Technically, I shouldn't let a sixteen-year-old boy even smoke in the first place. Just be nice to this one and—"

"—So," Karen said. Devon was startled by the way she plopped at the end of the bottom bunk. "What's your deal?"

He stepped away from the door and closer to Karen, but he didn't say a word.

"Come on now, don't be a pussy," she said. "My parents decided to leave me by myself in a crib, so they could get drunk while I slept. They didn't pay a babysitter, and they never returned home."

"How long have you been here?" Devon asked.

"I dunno. Since I can remember. I know someone else must've taken care of me for a few years. What's your story?"

"My parents forgot about me," Devon mumbled.

All at once, the bedroom door opened, Zach returned, Karen guffawed and shrieked on the bottom bunk, and Cindy asked for the three of them to have fun. She also added, "And Karen . . . back in your room by eleven." Then Cindy was gone, but Karen still laughed.

"What the hell's wrong with you?" Zach asked her once the door closed. "You high or something?"

Zach glowered at Devon and asked, "You been flirting with my girlfriend?"

Devon turned white, his lips and limbs tucked tight.

Zach grinned and said, "Jesus, this kid." He turned to Karen, who was at the end of her giggle fit. "You believe his face? You need to relax, man."

"He said his parents forgot about him," Karen shouted before losing herself to laughter again.

"I'm serious," Devon yelled. The room fell silent and he added, "I think something bad must've happened to them."

"Hey man," Zach replied. "They might be okay and still out there." Soon Zach joined his girlfriend in laughter.

"If they're alive, maybe Miss Cindy will somehow let them know I'm here," Devon said.

"You don't understand, man," Zach said. "It doesn't work like that."

"Look at me," Karen joined in. "The only thing I remember is here. No one said they were related to me. No one wanted to take care of me. No one's tried to adopt me. My sixteenth birthday is next month. How old are you, Devon?"

To be honest, Devon wasn't sure. He remembered his twelfth birthday at home, though it felt more like a formality on his family's end. He remembered his thirteenth birthday before the fishing trip incident. "Almost fourteen," Devon said. "Maybe."

"At least you're lucky you won't spend as much time here as I have."

"I mean, you kind of just stay here until you can go out on your own. No one comes back for us. That's why we're all here in the first place," Zach said.

XI.

For the next week or so, Devon didn't say much to Zach and Karen, and for the most part, they were rarely around. The only time he noticed them was when they'd stumble back into the bedroom, laced with cigarette smoke and possibly alcoholic drinks. While the two of them played in their own little world together, Devon used the time to explore the building and acclimate himself.

He dropped by the living area to browse the bookshelf. There were dozens of books—more than Devon had—but none of them interested him. He tried to crack open book after book, but even the words failed to make sense. It was as though all these stories were scribbled down to fill the space between the cover art on the front and the author's photograph on the back.

Once he surrendered the notion of finding a decent book, Devon wandered to the outside grounds, where younger children dispersed as the sun began to set. Along with nightfall, he expected more of the older children to head outside, but most of them didn't.

Since no one stood in his way or chased him off, Devon headed towards the corner of the building where he first saw Zach and Karen smoking.

In the far corner of the building sat a pile of browned cigarette butts stacked high enough to serve as a make-shift monument to the older children's unrelenting pursuit of rebellion. Just the idea had Devon thinking. If they were children outside of society, then they really didn't need to follow its rules. Rules were what kept those who belonged belonging. Yet Devon didn't feel he was quite there. He wasn't out of the circle; he was left behind by an honest mistake.

Nevertheless, his curiosity towards the insurgence kept him nosing around. A few feet away from the butts were a few broken bottles atop of a rain-soaked pile of leaves. He scattered the debris with his feet and stood flabbergasted by the sight of an old storm cellar door.

At an unobservant first glance, Devon didn't think much of it. It was simply interesting until he saw its poor construction. Old plywood made up the door—plywood which matched that of the broken seesaws and sandbox. The handle appeared to be nothing more than a swing's turnbuckle.

On rare occasion would Devon disobey his initial instinct, but it had been so long since he explored a new area quite as fascinating as this one.

He pulled the door open by its rusted handle and looked at the staircase. Now that he knew what lied underneath, he needed to know what lied beyond the stairwell.

Cigarette smoke and other odors indescribable to Devon rained out of the cellar with each cautious step he made towards the bottom. He felt the fierce chill from the concrete flooring tingle through his feet and legs.

Though he expected more, the cellar was only a cellar, albeit a bit larger than he imagined. His interest in the cellar flat-lined until he heard Karen's laugh.

Parting layers of cobwebs that blockaded the east side of the cellar like police tape, Devon made his way to Karen, following only the sound of her chorus-like chortle and the drying attack of smoke. No sooner than he reached Karen, another aroma clung onto him.

Karen and a few other older children sloshed down various drinks from half-full bottles and scowled at the aftertaste.

"Hey stranger," Karen spat out. "What brings you down here?" She held a clear bottle in one hand and smoked a cigarette with the other. The bottle was labeled vodka, but the brand was written in some other language. "It's Russian vodka," she added after catching his gaze.

"Is that . . . good?" Devon uttered.

"What? Seriously, what're you twelve?"

"Thirteen. Almost fourteen. I think."

Karen stepped back and leaned towards the floor as though someone pulled her by her dark hair. "Of course it's good. It's Russian vodka."

"How the hell did you get down here?" Zach broke out of the darkness, where two or three other teenagers began to doze off, dog-piled, in the corner. "Kevin, what're you doing down here?"

"It's Devon," Karen interrupted. "And he can hang out with us if he wants."

"Man, I swear if anyone else finds out—You're not going to rat on us, are you?"

Devon shook his head.

"See," Karen said. She pushed the bottle against Devon's chest. "If you wanna hang out here, you gotta take a swig."

Knowing no other way to get along and stay downstairs, Devon grabbed the bottle by its long neck and angled it far too high above his head, letting the vodka burn his throat.

∞

His eyes burned more than his throat when he awoke. The blanket of smoke had dissipated, and all that remained were quarter-full bottles on the cold concrete. As he disambiguated the cellar, Devon saw Zach sprawled out near the other teens.

Karen withdrew the last cigarette from her pack and brought flame to the end of it. With slumped lips weighed by disdain, she passed the cigarette to Devon.

"Honestly," he said, "I already feel like I'm going to die."

"That's exactly what this is for," she said. "It helps."

Shaking his head, Devon snatched the cigarette by the filter and inhaled too long of a drag.

As he coughed and shoved the cigarette back in Karen's hand, she said to him, "Besides, you'll only be dead if Cindy finds you missing."

Devon tried to jump to his feet in panic, but when he did so, he teetered by the wall where Karen leaned. Instead of rushing back to his room, he joined her and tried to calm down. Both of them soon slid down and sat on the floor. "What do we do?" he asked.

"Nothing," Karen said. Though the smell and taste of tobacco were far from alluring, the way she romanticized a cigarette was addicting to Devon. "We've still got a couple hours. Wanna another drag?"

Devon shook his head. "Why do you smoke?"

"Because it's pretty fuckin' awesome," she replied before putting the butt out in a crack along the floor. "What else is there to do?"

Devon was still cautious of his words, yet couldn't help but stay blunt: "If you've been here so long, how come you didn't smoke then? You're not even eighteen."

"I will be before you know it, and then I get the boot."

"That might actually be nice for you," Devon said.

She smiled. "You're so sweet. Tell you, though, I just hope I don't meet my parents out there."

"I thought—"

"—No," Karen said. "I just tried to convince myself they were dead. Look, I dunno how else to say this, but your parents are fine. I mean, they left you. Hopefully yours weren't like mine."

Devon pondered for awhile, despising the mere insinuation that his family could've been so sinister like Hugo Frankenstein at the site of his creation.

While a slight frustration built up inside of him, Devon could tell Karen felt more sorrow than he. He said to her, "I'm sure you'll be fine without ever meeting them again."

Karen started to smile, and then started to cry. Without any forewarning, she swooped in and forced Devon's lips open with her own. It was brief, shy kiss flavored by alcohol and tarnished by smoke, but it still put walls around the boy and the girl, separating them from the rest of the world.

XII.

When Devon awoke the next morning, his back *popped* and cracked from stretching out across the cold floor of his room. Zach rested next to Karen in the bottom bunk, still lost in the center of an alcohol induced dreamscape. Such rest never came to Devon. His dreams were ambiguous after the fact, and he couldn't recall how he returned to the room. All he could remember was the kiss from Karen.

Like clockwork, Karen rolled over to the edge of the bed and observed Devon with a crooked, tired stare. "Hey there. How was your night?"

"How . . . How did I get here?" Devon asked.

"Zach helped you up here. You were way gone."

"Did we?"

"Yes, but it was late and we were drunk, you know?" Though she said those words, her facial expressions disagreed with a contorted smile.

Devon couldn't believe how quickly the happiest moment in his life could've been dismissed. A person could show you who you really were in an isolated moment of sheer joy and attack you the next day with it like a weapon.

Quite honestly, Devon wanted to yell. He wanted to plead. He wanted to hear that last night was the best night of both of their lives. The reality remained that the greatest moment of someone's life could've quite easily been the biggest regret of someone else's. And this Devon feared, so he retreated into silence and closed his eyes.

∞

Devon tasted his own blood long before his eyelids flapped back, and before he felt a midday haze, he felt a calloused collection of knucklebone tearing through his lips and drilling through his teeth.

"You stupid, ugly fuck," Zach yelled down at him, spit spraying through the gaps of his teeth. "Get up."

In false hope the unexpected conflict would end as soon as he rose to his feet, in the erroneous presumption the two of them could remedy the situation through constructive conversation, Devon abided Zach's request. Seconds after he did so, Zach sent him back the ground with a heated left swing.

On the floor of their shared room, Devon rubbed his jaw line and spat out a gelatinous mixture of phlegm and blood. Inside of him, a batter of hatred churned, yet when he stood back up he never retaliated with a punch of his own. Instead he replied, "Why?"

Fist cocked and eager to connect with Devon's right eye, Zach stopped and said, "Did you seriously ask me why?"

Devon said nothing.

"Why? Hell, maybe Karen can explain it better." He turned to face Karen, who quivered with the bed covers wrapped around her body as some sort of emotional shield.

"Come on, Zach," she muttered, "it was nothing. We were drunk."

"Are you a slut?" Zach asked her.

"What?"

"Are you a fucking whore?"

Karen shook her head.

"Then this asshole took advantage of you."

She couldn't reply with anything more than a forced whimper. At this, Zach swung again.

Blood trickled down from Devon's eye as he plummeted to the cold floor mere seconds after he stood up.

"You stupid son of a bitch," Zach roared as he hunched over Devon and swung haphazardly.

As Devon began to cry out, the bedroom door flung open, and Cindy rushed to the center of the room. Though she and a few others worked to separate the boys, Zach's punches kept raining down, leading to a parallel between Devon's worldview and consciousness. To the boy, both were blurred and fading away.

XIII.

Cindy had no other choice than to relocate Zach after the quarrel to a place where his outbursts of violence could've been more controlled, if not subdued. Even after the fight, Devon still missed him.

Now as Karen's seventeenth birthday approached, she was the only person he could relate to and confide in. For awhile after her sixteenth birthday, though, Devon felt completely alone. For months at a time,

Karen wouldn't speak to Devon. The day before her birthday, however, Karen met Devon outside, where he helped Cindy with chores, and she said, "I'm sorry," before she started tearing up.

Cindy cocked her head to the side and analyzed Devon and Karen as they exchanged impatient glances. She said, "Why don't I leave you two alone for a moment?" And she walked back inside the building.

XIV.

The night before Karen's eighteenth birthday, she and Devon snuck out of the house into a thick fall thunderstorm with all the garnishes of a swollen sky followed by split-second thunder. Before the two of them closed the back door quietly, lightning webbed through the sky and ran away at the sound of quick rumbles. Devon swore the thunderbolt struck right outside the door, but they continued anyway.

Besides, Devon knew this would be the last night he'd see her. Though he'd never know until Karen admitted it, he wanted this night to be one more isolated moment of true happiness.

Around the house, battered streets and cracked sidewalks led to nowhere in every direction. Streaks of yellow and violet crossed the horizon as they headed east. Devon felt his shoes dampen and the puddle water seeping in through the netting at his toes.

The chill of the water soon elevated to his shins, rendering every fast step painful and as though his legs splintered against every dip in the sidewalk. Devon slowed down to favor his left leg, but he never stopped. He asked Karen, "Where are we going?"

She halted for a moment and surveyed what little they could see. "To the left, I think."

The two of them ran to the left, further into the black cast of the storm. Karen led Devon off to a small park. The entrance was a mile-long trail that ended at the center of the park, where there were three small pavilions with benches underneath.

Karen checked for the center pavilion for any puddles before she plopped down on the bench. She pulled Devon over by his arms and made him join her.

"I'm sorry how I treated you about the whole Zach thing. That night in the cellar really meant something to me," she said.

"Yeah, me too," Devon replied.

"Can we have a re-do?" Karen smiled and leaned in as the black sky crackled above the center pavilion in celebration.

∞

In the morning, Devon awoke in a shiver. He must've fallen asleep in his clothes, which were still damp. Though Karen's absence from his side brought doubt about the previous night, Devon assumed from a sweet fragrance on his pillow that they survived the bulk of the storm and returned to his room.

As a light thunder whispered above the house, He remembered what was going to happen on this day. Karen's eighteenth birthday. Irrespective of clumsy teeters as he rushed to the window, he made it across the room and pressed his face against the glass. Trying not to flinched as the wind whipped the window, he watched down below, where Karen packed her things into the trunk of a taxi.

She had arrangements for her first job out of the house and an income-based apartment waiting for her. Cindy hopped into the backseat, while Karen took in every inch of the house one last time.

Devon realized, now, she was right. The house wasn't a place where you waited to reunite with your family. It was just limbo.

Her eyes caught his, and she flashed him one last smile before she entered the taxi. Seconds later, Karen left without the slightest utterance of goodbye.

XV.

The next two and half years flew by before Devon was off to create his own space in the overbooked world. A cold spring breeze brushed his shoulders. He shook off the chill and placed a lidless box of books into the trunk of a taxi. He slammed the trunk closed and forced at smile at Cindy, who stepped into the other side. She waited for Devon to do the same.

Without hesitation, the taxi cruised down the highway once Devon sat down and buckled up.

"Are you excited?" Cindy asked him.

"Huh?" the taxi driver asked. "About what?"

"Not you," Cindy said. "I'm talking to the boy."

"Oh. Sorry."

Devon sighed and nodded.

"Hey, cheer up. I know you still miss Karen, but she's just the first girl you met. There'll be so many more out there, waiting for your charm." Cindy nudged his side.

"Yeah," the taxi driver said, "but guys like you and me, kid, we gotta have a whole lot of that charm."

"Would you mind your own business?" Cindy asked the driver. "Way to encourage the boy. Anyway, Devon, you're really gonna enjoy having your own life. That job—what is it again?"

The rubber against pavement provided an uncomfortable ambience to their broken conversation. After a bit, Devon said, "You know what it is. You arranged it."

"I most certainly did not." Cindy crossed her arms. "Giving you a good lead is not arranging it. C'mon, where are you working?"

"I have no clue," he said. "I don't even know how I got the job. I guess I'll be writing information for a phone book."

"That'll be fun," she said. "You'll get paid to write. With all those books you have, you should like being on the other end of the story."

"This is just boring phone book stuff."

"Yes, but it could be a start." Cindy uncrossed her arms. "And you'll have money to go out and have fun. It'll be a lot better than that cellar."

"You knew about that?" Devon cocked his head and grinned.

"Oh, of course. I'm a little slyer than you think. But hey, you'll get to celebrate your twenty-first birthday in downtown Long Brooke. You'll meet tons of new people. It'll be exciting for you, I promise."

∞

The next hour dragged on, and consequently, both Cindy and Devon breached their limit of things to say to each other. Static from the radio and road noise staled the air around them, and though Devon wasn't ready for a new life, he drew eager to escape the dreadful taxi ride. Cindy had always been so kind, he felt. However, he didn't want to ever remember the house, especially Karen.

By the time they arrived at Joy Apartments, the landlord awaited them near the front entranced. Cindy paid the cab fare and led Devon to the woman.

Devon stared up as he inched near the entrance of his new place, admiring the way the sky couldn't decide whether to rain or shine.

"Miss Miller," Cindy greeted the landlord while Devon lagged behind. She reached back and nudged the boy forward. "And this is Devon, your new resident. Like I said, I'll pay whatever he needs upfront, like a deposit . . ." Cindy continued to talk as the two of them headed to the office at the end of a long strip of apartments.

Devon waited behind and looked around him. Nothingness stretched out in all directions, and the apartments were the only ones off the interstate.

∞

Devon spent the rest of the day arranging what little furniture came extra with the room: a small desk with a bookshelf around it, a worn twin bed, a TV stand, kitchenette, and an old blue sofa which stood out in the maroon and white room.

With hesitant steps, Devon walked by an alarm clock that read 8:15PM, and answered the door. "You mind if I see what you've done with the place?" Miss Miller asked from outside.

XVI.

Every day feels about the same, Devon thought as he strolled down a list of phonebook clients (particularly the white and yellow pages) and called them all one-by-one. If they didn't answer, their number was reinserted into the number bank. If the wrong person answered, he offered them a hollow apology and tried to squeeze as much information out of them as possible. On the rare occasion the correct person actually answered, the conversation would always be the same.

"Hello, sir," Devon would say. "How's your day?"

Generic reply and repeat. Unless he encountered a real talker. Then the goal was to make them stop.

He'd take their information and charged them for continual placement in the book.

Devon didn't feel a thing. Today all he could think about was Joy Miller, his landlord. Months into his new residence, she *checked* and *checked* on the apartment. Now she always waited for him after work. Still, he didn't feel anything.

Somehow Devon made it through the entire call list for the day, and for the people and business that didn't answer, he'd call them first thing the next morning he worked.

Tomorrow was Sunday, he figured he wouldn't work on Sundays, but like every other business, they were open seven days a week, even during most holidays. No one was safe from a telemarketer such as himself. The trick was to convince someone you weren't soliciting.

And in spite of how he felt—or in this case, didn't feel—he could always meet company goals. All he remembered for a single day was the tick of an old clock at the far end of the cubicles. Finally, it ticked 6:00PM.

Devon sped to the punch clock where entered his badge number and placed his hand over a scanner.

Then it was a long drive down a short road on a drizzling Saturday evening.

By the moment he fussed with his apartment keys, Joy Miller greeted him from inside his own apartment. "I hope you don't mind," she said to him.

It didn't matter so long as she waived late payments with the promise of paying his next month's rent. "Not at all," Devon replied.

Tonight, like most nights, the two of them stayed in and watched late-night movies on a TV she donated to him. She scooted closer and closer. Shielded by each other's arms, they moved no closer. On occasion, Joy stared at the side of Devon's face, which he'd notice and smile back.

As the night drew long, Devon and Joy snuggled with one another on the couch. She yawned, and before she dozed off, she said, "Let's go out tomorrow night."

Joy soon fell asleep, but Devon never answered. Instead, he leaned in and followed suit.

∞

A piercing yellow ray cut through the blinds and burned at the center of Devon's closed eyelids. He slowly came to and slid Joy's head off of his arm. She fidgeted for a moment, and then she clutched a pillow and fell back asleep. Devon slipped off of the couch and turned off the TV. Next, he checked his alarm clock beside the bed: 6:45AM.

"Damn it," he muttered seconds before he scuttled around the apartment and prepared himself for work.

He brushed his teeth last and looked back at Joy on his way out of the bathroom, to the door. It didn't matter if she slept on his couch all day. She would be there when he returned home anyway.

∞

Every second of the work day felt like an exact clone of the last and the next. *Research each paid entry and call the one's that didn't match.* That was, of course, until he neared the end of his list. He normally filtered through old businesses or deceased owners, but the last name on one of the old records made him backtrack: Harrington. Thomas Harrington.

Devon checked over both shoulders and jotted down the most current information on Mr. Harrington and a previous address. The old entry was for his services as a live-in home caretaker.

∞

Joy met Devon at his front door wearing a bright pink dress with faded yellow flowers. The smile she flashed was contagious and involuntary. The kind of smile you couldn't restrain.

Part of Devon urged him to walk past her and pretend like he didn't remember what she said the previous night. Instead he said, "Where did you want to go tonight?"

∞

On the outskirts of Long Brooke stood a restaurant much smaller than the rest. It might've been one of the least beautiful buildings in Long Brooke from the sidewalks, but it took Devon back as soon as he stepped foot inside.

Dozens of small tables and booths laced the walls and center of the main room. Dozens of couples and groups whispered away until even a scream couldn't penetrate the white noise. A young woman greeted them at the entrance and seated them at a tiny round table near the front, where Devon faced Joy.

He never paid too close attention to her, but now he realized how much older she looked than the women around them. Instead her bangs were lined with silver and matted against her wrinkled forehead. Her blue eyes appeared gray under direct light. Her cheeks were pale and sunken in. All this didn't mean Devon found her less beautiful; it meant she was older. Soon enough, he'd forgotten about Joy as he admired the view of Chase Lake and roadside tree line akin to a dinner plate garnish.

When he returned his attention to Joy, she was halfway through a sentence: ". . . such slow service. Well, I guess it gives us a little time to chat. Tell me something I don't know about you, Devon."

"I dunno," Devon replied. For a moment, he was distracted by a young brunette server heading their way from the kitchen.

"Oh c'mon," Joy said. "No high school memories or anything?"

"Not really," he said. "What do you mean?"

And the server drew closer.

Joy rolled her eyes and scoffed. "I mean like a magical late night. A winning touchdown. Hell, a book you really liked."

"I was kinda home-schooled." Devon stood up and *clunked* his knee against the table under the chime of dancing silverware. He added, "Hold on just a second, Joy." He headed towards the server to take a closer look. "Karen!" he greeted the server with open arms.

She fell into them and said, "Oh my god, Devon! What are you doing here?"

Devon glanced back and tipped his head in Joy's direction. "I'm here with a friend. Her name's Joy."

Halfway out of his arms, Karen asked, "A friend, huh?"

"Yeah, she's my landlord."

"So you guys aren't like dating or anything?"

"I don't think so," Devon replied.

Karen shoved him forward and stormed off back for the kitchen. "That's good. Really great. I'm happy for you. I have to get back to work. I won't bug you two."

Before she reached the kitchen doors, Devon could hear her sob and rushed after her.

Another server cut in front of Devon. He said, "Sir, this area is for employees only. Please take your seat."

"I know Karen," Devon told the server.

"I'm sure you do," he replied. Now a manager joined his side.

Devon knew how Karen was. He needed to cheer her up as soon as he could, so he dodged both men and sprinted for the kitchen.

∞

Devon's lips didn't stop bleeding for around an hour after security had to throw him out. By the time he stopped tasting his own blood, he and Joy were already back at the apartment.

"Are you ready to tell me what happened?" Joy asked in a tone too soothing for such a perfect night gone to waste.

"Nothing," Devon muttered with one finger teasing the cut across his bottom lip. "Am I still bleeding?"

"Not unless you keep playing with it." She sighed. "Now are you going to tell me what happened?"

Devon rummaged his front pocket and felt a crumbled up piece of paper. He pulled out the note and stared at it. "I have to go, but I'll explain later." He started for the door.

"No," Joy said. "Tell me now."

He flashed the address at her. "This is where I'm going. I really need to go."

"Tell me what happened today." She stepped closer to him.

"Nothing happened," Devon said.

"So you just decided it would be fun to chase down that skanky cashier?"

Devon slammed his fist into the wall off to his right. "'Skanky cashier,' what the hell does that mean? Who the hell do you think you are?"

"What does *that* mean?" Joy asked, her voice brought to a boil.

"What do you think it means? Look at yourself. You're just an old, lonely woman."

"Who the hell do *you* think *you* are?! You're a goddamn pig. And you know what? The worst part is you have no right to be. Jesus, when was the last time you looked at yourself in the mirror?" Joy yanked her purse off of the floor and removed a pocket mirror. She opened it and shoved it towards Devon's face. "You ain't no big prize."

For the first time in awhile, Devon stared at every last detail of his face. His jaw line was too strong and too square. His teeth were yellowed and crooked. His eyes were blue but so dark and tired they came off black. His forehead displayed uneven wrinkles from the constant muscle strain of his dominant brow. These weren't details; they were deformities. He lost control of his breath for a fleeting moment upon realizing he was a monster.

"That's right," Joy said. "Take it in. I was so kind and caring to you. And for what? You're some cold-hearted, deformed little boy, and that's all you'll ever be."

As she finished, silence slipped through as the door slammed shut behind the boy. The boy walked towards a taxi with the slip of paper in hand. Though a bit late, the butler should've been home.

XVII.

Seconds before midnight, the taxi dropped the boy off in front of Thomas Harrington's home under a light rain. The boy paid his fare and tapped on the yellow roof of the car. As the driver sped off down the road, the boy neared the driveway, where he stole his first good look at the property. A lightly stained picket fence encompassed the outskirts of the yard, keeping some unwanted guests from ruining the even, dark grass. A light smoke derived from the chimney of the three-story home.

The boy kept walking down the driveway, following the thick essence of chimney smoke. He admired a small pond with a mini-geyser along the way until he reached the front door.

Crickets played Marco Polo so erratically their songs devolved into something plaintive and agitating, like a nearby whisper he couldn't quite discern. The perpetual ambient melodies from the woods an acre or so behind the Harrington Residence seemed to follow the twitter of the stars spread across the night sky. It was a shame someone so neglectful as the butler could forget to serve the boy and furthermore return home without a care. What would the boy's parents think? Soon enough, the boy knew he'd get his answers.

The boy took one more step forward and knocked on the front door with a peculiar sharpness like a snare drum. He could almost hear his dry knuckles crack against the windswept wood. For a few minutes after the knocks echoed off, he stood alone and drowned out by the chorus of nature. As the boy started to turn away and head back to his apartment (if it was still available to him at this point) with his chin rested on his chest, a sharp *creak* came from behind the house.

Around the east corner of the house, the boy watched as Tom snuck through a screened patio door. The butler glanced both ways, as though crossing a busy street, and headed for a black car in the driveway with light steps.

"Where are you going?" the boy asked while stepping closer to Tom.

Tom rested his hand against his brow as the security lights turned on. "Who is that?" the butler asked. He started forward, but he froze at the sight of the boy. "Devon?"

"Why did you leave me?"

Tom fidgeted in place and soon replied, "I didn't leave you until the house was sold." He reached into his coat and withdrew a handgun. With the barrel aimed at the boy, though with a shaky hand, he added, "Get away from me. I don't owe you a damn thing, so get off of *my* property or I'll have to use this thing."

The boy stepped closer. "Where are my parents?" he asked.

Mud splotched the corner of his shoes with each step. For the first time, the boy felt like he delivered all the weight of an eighteen-year-old, the weight of a man.

Gun still shaking, Tom said, "They're not *here*."

"That's not what I asked," the boy said as he drew nearer to Tom.

Tom couldn't control himself, and the gun wobbled in his hand. When his quiver evolved, the handgun slipped from his sweaty palms. Tom measured the boy and then eyed the gun a few feet in front of him.

The boy picked up the gun and stepped face-to-face with the old butler. "Why did you leave me?"

Tom sprinted off until he slid along the mud in the front yard and braced himself as he fell mere inches from the pond. He struggled to get to his feet, but soon enough the boy had the barrel of the gun between his eyes. "Please," Tom pleaded, "I didn't want to do it. They made me. Your parents made me.

"Look, they *said* I'd never spend another day as a servant as soon as they were settled in. You're too young to understand now. You might say you wouldn't do something just for money, but when you're an adult you'll be surprised what you *won't* do for money."

"They paid you to feed me in the room?" the boy asked.

"Look, Devon, they left you. Why would you wanna find them? Look at you, boy. You came together all right by yourself."

The boy pressed the gun harder against Tom's head. "Where are they?"

"They're not here," he swore.

"Tell me where they are."

Underneath the push of the gun barrel, Tom tried to scoot back, but slid along the ground with the extra force. His head smacked the side of the pond's concrete base, and all at once, his eyes rolled back and he was quiet.

The boy shook his head and tossed the gun into the pond. He stared at the back of the house and saw a light flicker upstairs.

XVIII.

The evening mist soon mutated into something denser and menacing, like some phantom curtain cutting the boy's life into slivers of what used to be and wide slices of what was to come. His feet *sloshing* along the muddy lawn and *squeaking* along the porch, the boy headed for the front door and then inside. A sweet aroma of vanilla candles drifted towards him. He not only smelled the fragrance, but he also could feel it. His flesh ached as he remembered the game of hide n' seek along the overly decorated third floor hallway. The boy remembered the first time he kissed Karen; how he'd hid in the cellar, away from any outside suspicion. And suddenly, the boy no longer wanted to hide. He marched into the kitchen and stopped at the stove.

For a moment, the boy considered the stove panel. He cranked up all the gas knobs but lit no flame. Without a second thought, he moved on for the staircase.

A repetitive melody spewed from the upstairs—a bedroom at the west end of the hallway. There, the boy stopped in front of the bedroom door and watched the light wave around his shoes. If he'd blinked, he would've missed the humanoid shadow moving along the taupe carpet. The boy studied the shadow, and when it disappeared, the boy propelled his entire body into the door until it opened wide.

Before he could make it inside the bedroom, the boy heard a loud *smack* against the door, and felt a force slip from underneath, as though a mole burrowed underfoot. A few inches away from the door, a much older Joan favored her right elbow.

She was the little sister he remembered every night since he was locked inside the bedroom. While she stared with a hi-beam gaze, the boy noticed her features. Her hair possessed a hay-like quality to it, and her eyes were a bright green with almost geometric blotches of blue. At the sight of him, her flesh drained itself of color; lastly, from her puffy lips.

"Devon?" Joan's lips shaped, although the boy wasn't sure if she actually said his name. "Is that you?"

"Joan?" the boy replied with a playful hint of mockery.

"I can't believe you're here," she said. "We never thought—I never you thought you'd return. They all acted like I was crazy. They had me convinced you never existed, like an imaginary friend."

"Imaginary friend?" he asked.

"I'm so glad you're alive, Devon," she said.

The way she added the boy's name brought warmth, a literal heat rushing throughout his body. Sometimes Devon felt like two different people: Devon, the young man some loved, and the boy who some had forgotten. Devon had little time to enjoy such relief once he heard the thunderous slam of a car door followed by another.

He looked at the bedroom door lock and noticed his parents had taken the same precaution of reversing the knob. In one fell swoop, he slammed the door, locked it, and rushed downstairs.

He could still hear Joan screaming for (or at) him as he hurried into the kitchen, where the smell of gas hovered above. Now all he needed was a flame.

By the dining room table, he saw a small lighter resting on the end chair. On his way over to the retrieve it, the front door opened and served as a blockade of fate. For the first time since the accident in the old house, the boy stood flesh-to-flesh with his parents.

XVIV.

Both parents locked in place at the sight of Devon. Despite his worst intentions, he embraced an eerie joy from finally reuniting with them. He said, "Mom, Dad."

Neither parent responded for what felt like hours, which only fueled the wrath broiling inside of the boy. Finally, his father said, "Who the hell do you think you are?" A phrase so familiar to the boy now.

Any image of excitement from the boy's parents dispersed quicker than the lightest morning fog as it always had before. "It's Devon, your son."

His parents stepped aside for a moment and whispered to each other. The grandiose house filled with each syllable bouncing from open wall to open wall without taking any more of a form. Their expensive dress shoes and heels *quacked* and *clacked* as they returned to the boy at the front door.

"My god, Devon," the mother said and rushed forward for a long-awaited hug. The father joined too, but once their heads rested on his shoulders, they began to sniff.

"What's that smell?" the father asked.

The boy panicked as his parents let go and stepped past him and into the kitchen.

"You. Are you—did you—are you trying to kills us?" The father chortled with such obnoxious bass in his tone. He withdrew a lighter from his pocket and handed it to the boy. "Go," he said, "burn us all down."

Lighter in hand, the boy vacillated.

"C'mon, try it," his father said.

The boy walked over to the stove and flicked the lighter, but halted. He looked back at his parents.

"Go on," the mother said.

The boy brought the lighter to the coils, and a fierce flame rushed up the vent. Soon, however, the flame hovered underneath the coils. All he managed to accomplish was lighting the stove. The heat pushed him back a few feet, but paled compared to the coil burn along his forehead as his father shoved him against the flame.

"You fuck up," the father said to the boy. "You can't get anything right. You're an untrained mutt that won't stop pissing on the carpet. But you know what? You bit us, so you know what happens when a dog bites its owner." He lifted the boy's head up for a second. "I'm just gonna end this now."

"No!" the mother yelled, but she was soon drowned out by the *crash* from upstairs. Joan jumped down the stairs, skipping them all, and sprinted into the kitchen. Without haste, she tried to pull her brother away from the flame, but her mother tossed her backwards, down onto the hardwood floor.

"Stay out of this," the mother told her daughter.

But Joan kept yelling, "He's real! He's a real person! Let him go!"

The father turned back and started to reply, "Stay out of this," when a group of police officers crashed through the house and brought both parents to the floor and latched handcuffs around their wrists.

XX.

Parents out of range now, the boy and his sister limped to the front yard, where the butler was being handcuffed. Near the mailbox stood Karen.

Joan by his side, the boy approached her and asked, "Did you call them?"

Karen shook her head and pointed to the butler with her emerald eyes. "I think *he* did. Maybe he confessed. I dunno. I just got here." With a slight chuckle she said, "How are things?"

The boy laughed too as one of the officers, a fit female, started to head their way.

"I guess everything's back to the way it was before. Maybe better if I wasn't so worried about her." He nudged his sister.

"Maybe she could stay with us," Karen suggested.

The police woman started to walk away with Joan.

The boy asked her, "Can I have a minute?"

She nodded and headed for the squad car with Joan.

"Us?" the boy asked Karen once the police woman and his sister were out of sight. "I figured you hated me now."

"I'm here, aren't I?" Karen asked.

"What do you mean?"

"I tried to find you again, but the woman at the apartment—the one you were with—said you were gone. She told me the address she saw you with."

"Cindy sure got me the right job," the boy said.

"I think Cindy's a bit more sly than we give her credit for," Karen said. "Anyway, I'm here because you are. I'm sorry about before."

Though he paid attention, the boy's head jerked to the side at the sound of a car door closing, and he was reminded of his bedroom door so many years ago. The image faded as the police woman made her way back towards him.

"So what'll you do if you get custody of her, your sister?" Karen asked.

The police woman clasped the boy's shoulder and said, "Come along, we have to bring you back to the station for now, to sort all this out."

"See you when I get out?" the boy asked Karen.

She smiled. "All three of us should go out together. It'll be fun."

The boy nodded.

As he started to walk away, the officer asked him, "So you got a name?"

"Devon," Karen called out from behind.

"Devon," the officer replied, "My name's Sarah. It seems like someone sure likes you."

Devon shrugged.

"You gotta appreciate things like that," she said. "You gotta appreciate beautiful things like that in this world, no matter how normal or small they seem."

Devon ducked down into the squad car and pulled Joan closer to his seat. "We're gonna be all right," he said to her in an attempt to wipe away her tears.

Underneath a crawling rain, the squad car drove off. Devon stole one last admiring glance of Karen and brought the natural smile back to his sister. For the first time since they reunited, Joan grinned back at him, and the boy rediscovered fire.

Façade

Nauseating strobes flash through the packed night club and break everyone down into static. My head spins as I try to focus on a blurred blond woman across from me on a curved leather bench. I watch her tap her neon-painted fingernails along the table.

With one hand running along the side of my head, she makes me recoil even before she flashes her cracked grin. This ghost of a woman digs her nails into her face and peels down her flesh. Rather than cartilage or tissue, underneath her skin is a deep blackness with only her eyes and bone structure to reveal.

Some sudden change in motion, I'm to my feet and stumbling backwards across the sticky floor, which is resonant of a good time gone wrong. She stays in her seat, sipping on an Amaretto Sour. She sets her drink on the table and lets the fluorescent liquid run along her jawbone and out of her throat. Rummaging through her handbag, the blond woman pulls out a pocket mirror and turns it at me.

Her sharp nails clench my wrist and pull me closer, until I can see my reflection in the mirror. From my forehead to the bridge of my nose, my flesh melts away, developing into a dark abyss much like hers.

∞

Akin to a knife in my chest, a stabbing pain flares my lungs with each rapid breath. I spring upright in my bed at the sound of a loud rapping. My heartbeat echoes around the room; the sound is thumping in my eardrums, as if it derives from my mind and not my heart at all.

Deep breaths through my nostrils, down into the bottom of my lungs, and out of my mouth, I focus in on silencing my erratic sounds. My heartbeat becomes nothing more than an unfamiliar drum in the background. I hear the knocking again.

A curious thought crosses my mind: *What if I pretend to be asleep; will it go away?* Parents tell their children if they sleep, the monsters will go away. Then there's Santa Claus and Freddy Krueger.

Twisting the sheets around my limbs, I roll over to face the brunette twins lying next to me, asleep.

Knock, knock, knock.

Sliding out of bed, careful as to not wake my beautiful guests, I tip-toe towards the door. No sooner than I crack the door open, Ray peers in. Twenty-seven, Ray is slightly taller than me (though certainly not in a way that emasculates me) and has a little too much salt in his pepper for being so young (though older than me). He slips his rectangular glasses further back on his nose, the side pads teasing his tear ducts. He wears an expensive dress shirt with ripped jeans.

Ray tries to barge in, but I push a stiff arm forward into his chest and shut the door behind us.

Underneath a lonely light in the hallway I ask Ray, "What do you want?"

"Mike," he responds, his eyes surveying the room through a small gap near the hinges. "What are you doing in there?"

"Trying to sleep," I assure him.

"You're awake now. C'mon, Mike, let's go outside."

Thick grease polishes the back of my left hand as I rub my forehead. "What time is it?" I ask him.

Ray glances down at his watch, a rare sight on most people after the ceaseless explosion of telecommunication devices. He keeps his watch clean —white and silver. "Like four," he says. "C'mon, let's go."

Pointing back at the bedroom door, I reply, "I've got these two twins here—"

"—I thought you were trying to sleep," he says. "Wait, twins?"

"I dunno," I admit. "They look like twins. Good enough."

"That's always your problem, man," Ray says. "You've always gotta have these bimbos around to prove—"

"—Save the speech, Ray."

I start to open the bedroom door, when Ray adds a little louder, "See, you've always gotta have these bimbos around—"

"—Ok. Fine. Let's go," I mutter and leave my lovely guests by themselves in my bedroom. You are the shit you put up with.

Outside Ray has a few beers ready for me, next to a pink .22. The deck faces a backyard stretching until it drops over the horizon. He leads me to the beers and the guns at the end of the deck. He hands me a cold one and the pink .22. Another .22, black, is at his feet.

Ray tucks his gun into his armpit with one hand and grabs the beer with the other.

Though I've never fired a gun before, I nestle the butt along my shoulder, which feels wrong.

Ray loads the gun, and a slight aroma of gunpowder fills the air.

"Jesus, Ray," I say. "You're gonna piss off the entire neighborhood."

He reloads and fires again. "It's relaxing," he says. He reloads.

Sighing, I load the pink .22 and follow suit. The slight recoil catches me off-guard, but I'm not shaken by it, although I expected to be. "Then tell me, why did you wake me up? Please say it's not just so we can shoot in the dark."

"Isn't that what we always do?" he replies. And fires.

The whisper of his gun is followed by mine. "It's gonna be one of those drunken,
philosophical kind of nights, isn't it? Mom used to love that about you, you know."

"Leave *that* alone," Ray says through clenched teeth. He aims.

"What's the point of dragging me out here, Ray?"

Without hesitation he says, "I've been thinking about *people* lately."

Though the last words on my mind, I say, "Fuck people."

He replies, "And look where *that* has gotten you."

"Better off than you are."

I slam the .22 down and walk for the backdoor, when Ray says, "Some people only need someone special to hold their hand and reassure them in times of doubt. And when they're confident and move on, sometimes they don't think twice about it all." Fires. Reloads.

"Man, spit it out," I respond. "I've got these two twins up there, and you're beating around the bush."

"That's redundant."

"What is?" I ask him. "It's just a turn of phrase."

"No," he says, "'two twins.'" Ray checks his gun to see if it's loaded. He fires. "Ever since I moved in— since Mom—you've had a different girl over every night." He gulps down the last of his drink. Reloads.

"You've got two seconds to step off," I shout and then recognize the unintentional volume of my voice. "I'd hate to kick my own brother out on the streets."

Ray fires his gun and says, "I'm not calling you a womanizer or anything; nothing like that. But I want to know exactly who *you* think *you* are."

I slide the door open and step inside the house. "Goodnight, Ray," I tell him.

"Wanna go to the park after we visit Mom tomorrow?" he asks at the last second.

Halfway to closing the door, I mumble, "Sure."

Ray fires two more shots as I enter the house to resume some overdue cuddling with two twins.

∞

The Long Brooke Park consists of six possible pathways along fresh-cut grass, tree-shadowed picnicking hills, and a small stream leading to a miniature waterfall underneath a photoesque bridge. Each pathway is a mile longer than the last, ranging from a mile to six. The more extensive pathways lead to a well-kept sidewalk, bike path, and in some locations, a small transcendental walkway.

The center of the park, by comparison to the outskirts, is a generic playground for both young romances by night and elderly couples by day. Save the bridge, nothing really stands out, and perhaps that is the reason Ray brings me here. That, or he figures I won't kill him in a public area.

Up ahead is a set of benches; around them, children play with toys or the picnic sets. A few people read, though not many. Joggers blast by on the longer path, leaving cold gusts in their trails.

Ray's dressed in the usual gear: torn jeans and a dress shirt. He says, "Look at all of them."

More joggers pass by, and soon to pass a little further behind is a redheaded jogger, who I follow with my eyes.

Ray adds, "All these people cluttering around this cookie-cutter park, smiling and playing with their kids. Kissing their loved ones."

"All I see is an epicenter of façades," I tell him. "All these people gossiping, pretending to listen to each other until it's their turn to speak again. Showing the world how much better their lives are than everyone else's."

"See, Mike, that's where you're wrong." He leans back on the bench and stares at the shapeless clouds. "These people *are* happy. They aren't playing face. They *are* listening to each other. There's love. There's friendship."

"There's a lot of bullshit," I counter. "Nothing about these people reveals anything true or worth knowing."

Ray turns his head towards me and replies, "People aren't going to project their flaws, you know. Of course they're gonna flaunt whatever makes them happy—what makes them feel significant."

The redheaded jogger nears the bench, her body glistening under a layer of sweat. She wipes away the grease from her face and adjusts her headphones at the bench next to us.

"Why don't you go talk to her?" Ray asks.

"And say what?" I ask him back. I can't imagine having anything in common with such a stunning woman. "What, talk about the weather? What's my plan? Besides, you're the one who thinks I'm a womanizer."

"I dunno," Ray says. "Just talk about exercise or something. Tell her you always see her jogging around here and wanted to say hello to a somewhat familiar face. I explicitly said you were not a 'womanizer.'"

"Step one, according to you, is lie. Step two is—what—approach her like a creep?"

"No, it's called breaking the ice."

"And then what?" I ask. "How do I introduce myself? How can I maintain conversation with her?"

"Just . . ."

"Nothing," I tell Ray. "Even if I talk to her, it'll be about the day or her appearance, or I'll laugh at one of her jokes, even if it's not funny. But I won't ever tell her a damn thing about me."

The redheaded jogger reties her shoes and pushes her ear buds in. At the sight of me, she smiles as she turns on her music, which I can hear clearly from my position on the bench. If I knew more about music, then I would have something to say. She stalls for a moment.

"Say anything, man," Ray insists. "We're all just people trying to be people."

"It doesn't matter," I respond. "Even if she and I hit it off, she won't ever know anything about me." The redheaded jogger passes by, music seeping out of her ear buds, and I can't peel my eyes off of her. She blurs into the sunlight somewhere beyond my view. "Ever," I repeat for emphasis as I rise to my feet and jog after the redhead.

∞

Her name is Sarah or maybe Cara. Perhaps even Patricia. She's the redheaded jogger from the park, and her hands roam along the fringes of my body. Nearly glued together, we stumble into my dark bedroom, isolated by the starlight peering in through the blinds.

Both of our faces appear flushed in the idle television screen across from my bed. She pulls my head towards her and runs her hands over the right side of my face. I sink in for a kiss, and we entangle in the sheets.

∞

After a quick snooze when we finish, I rub my head and look at Sarah, Lisa, Patricia, or maybe even Carol. The redheaded jogger who is deep asleep next to me, naked under twisted covers and dead to the world atop of tossed pillows. I stare up at the stucco ceiling until I pass out again.

∞

Into an unfamiliar bedroom, I carry two glasses of red wine, though I can't recall ever favoring the sharp tongue of it over hard liquor or other spirits. The floor distances itself from my feet, tunneling far below my toes. I realize my socks are the only thing I'm still wearing, and between the falling floor and the crooked entrance to the bedroom, it's obvious I've already drank my fair share.

Lucy, Linda, or Lexi—the redheaded jogger—awaits me, her bare nipples pressing against the silk sheets. Every fabric melts around her, as though it was designed for flattery and to compliment her figure from every angle. I gesture the glass, but she shakes her head.

Placing the glass on an end table, I slide under the covers next to her, socks still on. We toss and turn, never separating more than a few inches. She play-bites my lip over and over until it's numb, and I grunt and bite back, although nothing about pain turns me on. Then I taste the saltiness of blood.

She's pulling me closer. Sliding me towards her. I reach out for the side of the bed to grip on but knock her wineglass against the brass-base lamp. Glass shatters.

The redheaded jogger smiles and reaches over for the largest shard of glass. My reflection, upside down on the piece, glares back at me.

Her grin draws wide as she lifts the shard high above her chest and plunges it down, lacerating her flesh until the glass *thuds* against bone.

I'm falling off of the bed and convulsing. "Oh my god," I mutter. "What?"

The redheaded jogger stares down at her chest, watching the red river stain the sheets. With a worried smile, she looks at me and asks, "I've really done it this time, haven't I?"

Thwack! My back smacks against the cold tiled floor. *What bedroom floor is tiled?* I wonder.

Collapsing into a fetal position, I can't help but stare at the blood as it cascades over the edge of the bed and onto the floor, inching towards my face. The metal smell burns my nostrils, although I'm not one hundred percent positive I truly smell it.

The redheaded jogger asks, "I'm going to die from this, aren't I? Because I couldn't stop."

Soon the floor turns into a pond of her blood and floods like a basement after bad storm. The blood never quits flowing; instead, it currents and crimson waves crash along the shore-like walls.

I close my eyes and pretend I'm not drowning.

When I open my eyes again, the redheaded jogger stands up on the bed, dead and as though her nerves jerk her upright for me to see her body drying and cracking apart. Her shell falls to the saturated sheets. Underneath she is an older woman with a prominent brow and chin. She keeps aging, keeps aging.

"Mom?" I ask under my breath, spitting out some of her blood.

"Your mother's dead, my dear," she says.

I shake my head, confused. "You're her. You're dead."

The old woman grabs the red glass shard and runs it along the bed, laughing as it tears into the foam. At the edge of the bed, she hoists the shard above her head and jumps down to the floor, her chipped smile inches away from my bloody lips. She holds the glass above me and laughs.

∞

Like loose cargo against the side of a ship, my heart pounds against its cage as I spring upright in my bed. I check my chest for any blood or wounds. *None.* The redheaded jogger next to me is still beautiful, still young, and still alive.

I sigh.

She cracks her eyelids and mumbles, "Is everything all right?"

Instead of answering at first, I lie back down. The redheaded jogger is quick to sleep before I say, "Sure.

Everything's fine." My eyes want to lock shut as I'm ravenous for sleep, but all I can do is quiver.

∞

Long after the redheaded jogger leaves, I rush downstairs and barge into Ray's room without knocking. The room is a mess on the side closest to the door and immaculate around his desk, where a Beretta lies next to a photograph. At the sound of the door slamming shut, Ray snatches both items and shoves them into the desk.

"Sure, man," he says, "come right in."

I plop on the recliner next to his desk. "It's my house," I remind him.

He says, "Guess you're right." There's something distant about his tone.

"You okay?"

Ray stays silent. He withdraws the photograph from his desk and stares. It's a picture of him and his ex-wife Emily. Smart, beautiful in a way only the word beautiful can describe, and too selfish to stick around a man with baggage, as she so eloquently told him before she disappeared. "I was thinking about what you said at the park," he almost whispers.

"Man, don't listen to me. I've just been in a real funk lately."

"I think you're right, though. She waited around for a few months, but Emily *just fucking took off*. After Mom passed. And I can't stop wondering why."

"Whatever happened to her?" I ask.

"She just wanted to get away, I think," Ray responds. "Maybe she was learning too much about me."

"Forget her then. If someone really wanted to marry you, then they would've stayed with you no matter what, you know? You can't let some bitch get the best of you."

"And this is coming from *you*?"

"Yeah, and I'm your best friend, Ray. You can't get rid of your brother."

"Tell me something about that redhead you had in your room last night," Ray says.

I might've muttered, "Point taken."

Ray opens the drawer containing the gun. He holds the Beretta up, and I admire the gloss of craftsmanship. Mankind hasn't developed a good tool to preserve life, because what we really want is a sure-shit way to end it. "I bought this back before she left," Ray says. "Thought I might need it someday."

"Don't you dare," I say.

"Don't worry; it's not for me."

I give him a speculative stare. "You wanna know why I can't—"

"—Don't divulge your problems to me right now. I have enough of my own."

"I just thought—"

"—I'm nothing. I'm fine." Ray shakes as he picks up the photograph and turns it around again. This display of emotion is a bit much of Ray, and the rarity of the event captures me while my eyes ingest a story lost behind broken glass. "Just get out," he says.

One arm forward, I try to provide what I know as comfort, but he slaps my hand away from his shoulder and says, "Just leave me alone right now."

Though diffident, I walk over to the doorway. As I grip the handle, he asks, "Do you wanna go to the club tonight?"

I'm frozen, one hand still out in front of me. I reply, "Sure, man. Let's do that. Please don't do anything stupid, all right?"

He nods. "It's not me I'm worried about," he says.

∞

From our barstools we can see all of the clubbers have sex with clothes on, otherwise known as "dancing." The scene here is a melted series of silhouettes and vibrant colors with a complete stench of body spray and sweat, cigarettes, and regret. Drinks spill as the clubbers rub against each other and exchange desperate smiles.

I signal for the barkeep underneath the rain of neon lights. He waves his index finger "one moment" at me and finishes mixing drinks for a couple of women at the other end of the bar.

"What can I get for you fellas?" he asks when he finally arrives at our end.

Before we can order, Ray darts his head in the direction of the dance floor, where in the center of ecstasy and confusion, Emily moves around by herself.

The light above her brings Emily to focus, and Ray pursues.

I ask him where he's going, and he doesn't so much as look back at me.

"All right," the barkeep says, "What can I get for *you?*"

I order the safe and classy: Rum n' Coke.

The barkeep turns away to make the drink, when my attention centers on a brunette woman scooting closer to me. She arrives at the stool next to mine within a matter of seconds. "Don't tell me a handsome guy such as yourself is here by his lonesome," she says behind tectonic violet eyes and over-glossed lips.

"I'm with him," I say as my index finger searches for Ray.

She cocks her head and follows my gesture. "Who? I really can't hear you. Wanna go someplace with less noise?"

In day-to-day life, this is unacceptable behavior, but add a club and some alcohol and it becomes an act of courtesy. My lips shape "no" but the music drowns out any utterance of the word.

"What?" she yells over the music, her voice intoxicated by unnatural levels of estrogen.

The barkeep returns with the drink, and I say to the brunette woman, "Sure. After this drink."

∞

We crash onto a floating bed at the center of her studio apartment. It's at the top of a high-rise at the end of Lakeside, before the city limits of Long Brooke. Sweeps of flowery fragrance latticed by vanilla tosses along the walls. *Her pillows smell unusually clean,* I think as she tears my shirt open.

She begins to fiddle around with my belt, when a sudden urge to break away overwhelms me. In a flash, I see the redheaded jogger morph into the dilapidated woman. I slip to the edge of her bed and place my head into my palms. I swear I'm not weeping.

"What's wrong?" the brunette woman from the bar asks, although there is either a lack of sincerity or too much alcohol in her tone.

"I'm fine," I slobber out.

"Can we fix this?" she asks—not quite the question I thought she had in mind. Her voice is seductive despite its balloon-squeal pitch, and in a way, indescribable. Sometimes you have to hold a diamond to understand its beauty.

I rush up to my feet and collect my clothes, even though I confess part of me wants to stay. As I take off, I glance down at my cell phone and see a text from Ray: "Backyard. Now!"

On my way out, I swear I hear the brunette woman say, "Pig."

∞

My feet can't move any faster after I hear Emily scream from the backyard. As I turn the last corner, I find Ray holding his Beretta against the side of her head. She cries with her knees planted in the mud. Rain water glares off of the gun's steel.

"What the fuck are you doing, Ray?" I yell across the backyard.

"Don't make a scene out of this," he says.

"Please let me go." Emily whines and then sniffles.

"It's ok," Ray says, and I think he's talking to me. "You were right, Mike. This needs to happen."

"What needs to happen?" I ask between shallow breaths.

Ray replies, "We need to get rid of all the disguises. We've gotta stop these people from taking control of us. Fuck her.

"I never said that, Ray."

Ray cocks back the gun and teases the trigger. "You're right. These people have nothing to offer. They're all the same. All fakes."

He grabs Emily by the hair and lifts her to both feet. She slips along the mud. He holds the gun out towards me, and I step back. "You know best," Ray says.

"No," I tell him.

"Take the gun. Do this. It's right." He shoves the Beretta into my shaking hands.

I say, "I can't do this, Ray. What the hell is wrong with you, man? We can work this whole thing out."

Rays sends Emily down to the soggy ground with a violent shove, and pushes me forward once his hands are free. "Think of your life," he says. "Think about it. Mom left us. Emily left me. All these women want nothing to do with you. You were right when you said we can never really reveal anything about ourselves to anyone else."

"I was in a funk," I dispute. "That's all it was."

"Yeah, but think about it: Emily left me after Mom died. None of these women want to know their men, and maybe we don't want to deal with them either. But if we're pigs, what are they?"

For some reason, I contemplate the question.

His hand clasps over my own and tenses. His index finger guides mine to the steel crescent. "There's no point," he says. "So what if we get caught for this? At least we stood up for the right thing. Maybe people will learn to accept others for who they are."

"I don't think they'll ever learn," I reply.

"How else can we be sure?" Ray asks with a warped smile. He presses my hand even closer to the steel; my finger closer to the trigger.

Emily screams louder.

Ray says, "This is how we find ourselves. You were right, you're not a womanizer, but these sorts of people have taken our identities away from us. We have the meaningful lives, yet they decide whether we fit in. Do it, Mike. Shoot her."

Her eyes beg me to stop.

"Do it," Ray hisses.

I follow the trigger with my index finger, and Ray stops guiding me.

Blood must lace Emily's throat, the way she screams.

I drop the gun, and it fires into the woods. "I can't do it," I concede. Something comes over me— some force of animosity and bewilderment I cannot quite comprehend—and I begin to swing at Ray.

Emily rushes to her feet and steps between us, pushing us apart with her arms out in a cross. After a deep breath, she looks at Ray, and they both laugh.

"What the hell?" I ask.

They collect themselves. "God that was scary," Emily says to him.

Ray turns to me and says, "I was worried about you, man."

"Tell me what the hell is going on, Ray," I say.

Ray and Emily walk away, holding hands. He calls back, "I think you're figuring it all out." They leave me alone in the backyard underneath the clout of rain. As much as I want to shoot him, I want to laugh, and I can feel a grin slice across my face.

Until they stop.

Gunfire rumbles like thunder so immediate and loud I knew the lightning struck near.

To be continued . . .
in Ashland's Asylum.

Last Stop

They wanted money; not a life.

Around 2:30 AM, Lotus and Switch scuffed their heels against the jagged sidewalks of Raven's Crook. Underneath the black sky like molten tar, the two darkly-dressed men meandered with a certain dance of confidence in their steps.

Between the *screeches* of metal from the nearby train station, a switchblade clicked. Always playing with his antiquated blade, that's how Switch gained his name.

"Would you stop that shit, man?" Lotus asked.

Switch giggled and returned the knife to his front jean pocket. "Damn, dude," he replied. "We're good." He pointed at his eyes. "See these, man? These are as good as a bat's at night. I'll spot a cop from a time zone away."

"Yeah, yeah. Your superman eyes. Until someone fucking rakes those little beety holes of yours out. Then you'll really be fucked, and I won't have to hear anymore about your x-ray vision."

Another train soared by and hollered over Switch's response. Both of them glanced up at the train station and watched the lightning of metal against metal.

Stairs led from the station down to the potholed streets of East Raven's Crook, a place where no one risked walking alone at night. Such fear led to miscalculations, such as overlooking the bus stop a few hundred feet away from the stairs, near the unlit basketball courts. These mistakes were where Lotus and Switch came into play.

When the train passed, Switch muttered, "What's the plan?"

"I think we need to make a move," Lotus replied.

"Is that from the boss?"

Lotus belated a response, but intimidation didn't linger in his eyes. He soon said, "You misunderstand, Switch. There is no more boss. There's only you and me now. I say we make a hit."

Switch faltered as another train braked on the tracks overhead. The two of them hid somewhere in an alleyway near the staircase and waited.

II.

Warren reached for his cell phone when the automated voice came over the LA (Lakeside) train's intercom: "Last stop. Raven's Crook. All passengers must exit the train. Watch your step as you leave. Thank you for choosing Chase Lines."

"Christ," he muttered. "Raven's Crook?" He dashed to information desk after he left the train.

A woman with barbed wire hair rested her head against her palm. She wore a black and white suit, much like a flight attendant's, but she forgot to iron on her smile.

She maintained the same rubber gaze of disinterest as Warren stepped up to her desk. They traded glances, but neither spoke.

He tapped on her window, to which she barely twitched. When he reached out to tap again, his bare arm slipped from his dress shirt sleeve to reveal a long scar running up his arm. Along the scar were three tally marks tattooed in a heavy ink.

The woman spotted his arm and sat up.

Warren rolled his sleeve back down his arm.

She asked, "Is there something I can help you with?"

"Yes," he said. "I must've taken the LA train too far or something. I thought it would actually stop in Lakeside."

"Damn, honey," she replied with no sympathy in her tone. "The train left *from* Lakeside."

"But how come the other trains go *to* Lakeside?"

"It just depends when and where you take the LA train. You're a long ways from Lakeside. Why didn't you say something earlier? Damn, you're lost, aren't you?"

"I *kind of know* Raven's Crook," Warren replied, though his tone suggested he didn't.

The woman shook her head. She leaned forward and said, "No, you know *daytime* Raven's Crook. You can't *know* Raven's Crook at night."

"Fine. I don't know Raven's Crook. Is there another train I can take back?"

"Shit, honey, you're gonna hafta head up town. No train stopping here will take you to Lakeside, at least not for another couple hours or so."

"I don't have that kind of time," Warren said.

The woman replied "Then you're gonna hafta head up town by foot and find the next stop. Damn, why did you wait so long to ask?"

"Are there any taxis?"

She snorted as she laughed. "No moron drives around Raven's Crook 'round these hours." Worry resumed across her flattened lips.

Warren exhaled stress and started to head away. Before the information desk fell out of sight, he turned to the woman and asked, "What would you do?"

She snickered. "I would've paid more attention and never fucked up in the first place. I dunno what you're gonna do, but I'm gonna go home and try to not think twice about it. I don't wanna stay up all night, thinkin' some sap is roaming Raven's Crook alone and lost."

Warren's ears rang. His lips opened, but nothing came out.

"Shit, honey," the woman muttered, as she fell back into her chair. "Good luck. Damn."

III.

The line running downstairs from the Chase Line Station soon dissipated as passengers exited in couples, and then one-by-one. Train stations and other transportation areas were a terrific spot for Lotus and

Switch to pick out their unlucky *customers*—they weren't *victims* unless they chose to be.

Many traveled in protective company, although couples and groups were no better than a single individual—more pockets to be picked. But numbers did sometimes pose a problem, and Lotus recognized such a fact.

Even so, loners weren't always weaker. All too often, Lotus spotted individuals endowed with biceps twice the size of his handgun. Some of them strapped knives or guns to every limb.

"Who are we lookin' for, Chief?" Switch asked, his tone too cheery for Lotus.

Lotus slapped his partner against his head and said, "Shut up."

Switch rubbed his head. "Just wondering."

Lotus observed all the passengers with a fierce attentive stare. "I dunno. Someone alone."

"How about lost?" Switch asked, again too loud.

Smacking Switch once more, Lotus peered into the night. He didn't detect anyone lost. "Where?"

With his index finger pointed out in front of Lotus' eyes, Switch directed his boss' focus. "There."

Lotus sorted through dozens of passengers before he stopped on one—the last man off of the train.

IV.

Into the engulfing blackness, the screen of Warren's phone glowed. On display, a navigation device led the way until a quick flash of red erased it all.

"Shit," Warren said to no one in particular. "Not now."

With a dead phone, Warren stood between the dark streets of Raven's Crook, staring at all the turns, dead-ends, and alleyways with unintelligible names, faded with age and never retouched.

He searched the two main sidewalks along the center road. Streetlamps were as scarce as a much needed taxi, but from the colorful cast of the traffic signals, he saw a sidewalk leading to the next train station. Although it was difficult to determine, he figured the station stood only a few miles away.

Though the darkened streets of Raven's Crook shook him inside and out, Warren imagined he could evade any unfortunate meetings, and if that failed, the worst that could happen was death. Even that thought felt erroneous. There were worse things than death.

V.

Their victim—or customer, rather—stepped out in front of them.

Lotus pointed forward and Switch slipped out of the alleyway to follow the unfortunate soul.

Once the man came into clear sight, Lotus waved Switch out. Together, they scoped out their prey.

The customer stood no taller than six feet with a medium stature. Not to say he resembled a skeleton, he certainly couldn't do too much to protect himself. Lotus mouthed the word "Go."

Both men, still with their powerful strides, gained ground on the customer as he fiddled with his phone and jerked his head in the direction of every street sign.

VI.

For awhile, Warren fidgeted with his phone to send a faint warning to the men following him. He couldn't be sure they meant any harm, but in the event they did, they would know he could dial 9-1-1 within a moment's notice.

But if he was in their position, a phone wouldn't come off as much of a threat.

The thunder of a train guided his way. From where he stood, the dimness worried him. Worst of all, the two men still pursued him through every move. He used the screen of his phone like mirror glass to see them.

"Miss the bus?" one of them—a taller, broader man—asked.

The other kept silent, with one hand in his front pocket.

Warren ignored them and carried on.

"He asked you a question, man," the other—a smaller man—asked. "We're just tryin' to help."

"You look lost," the bigger one added.

Warren jabbed his thumb against the power button on his phone, each time hoping for enough battery life to call the police. Calling the police, however, could've proven to carry its own complications.

In the next moment there was both chaos and clarity.

The larger man stepped in front of Warren—a scraping noise coming from underneath his heels. "People always miss the bus. Damn guides don't always remember it's there."

Warren pivoted, but the smaller man stepped in his path. "Bet you wish you made the right turn and hopped onto that bus, huh?"

"Please guys," Warren said, "you don't want to go through with this."

"*We* don't want to go through with this?" The larger man stepped closer to him. "You mean, *you* don't wanna go through with this."

"Cash or we fuck you up, man," the smaller man said. Moonlight bounced off of an exposed switchblade and into Warren's eyes.

VII.

Their customer claimed he didn't carry any cash, which both Lotus and Switch assumed to be bullshit. Lotus reached for the gun tucked against his back.

"You really should reconsider," the customer told them.

"I was just thinkin' the same thing," Lotus replied. His fingers teased the cold steel.

"Yeah," Switch said, still playing with his blade. "Whatcha gonna do about it?"

The customer did the right thing and kept silent, although it also screamed he was weak.

"See," Lotus said, "you ain't gonna do shit."

"Yeah," Switch said. "Besides, man, I got eyes that can see a move before you even think it."

Lotus grew tired of all the needless conversation and provided the catalytic action of withdrawing his gun.

All in one fell swoop, the gun came into sight, the customer deflected with a kick to Lotus' chest before he stole the switchblade from Switch.

The customer jabbed the knife into Switch. Next he snagged the handgun and aimed at Lotus' forehead. For them, the night drew twice as dark as before.

VIII.

When he awoke, Lotus fought to disambiguate his location. Somewhere in the unlit room, he could hear Switch. The sound was familiar to Lotus: weeping.

As Lotus looked around, a dim light flickered on in front of him, illuminating an old building foundation, which in Raven's Crook could've meant they were anywhere.

A thin layer of water crossed the concrete floor, providing Lotus no more knowledge than any other detail, until the red cloud traveled to his feet.

At the other end stood the customer, his arm sliced open; showing Switch his own knife.

The customer finished running the blade along his own arm and licked off the blood. He said, "There's something to admire about old-fashioned tastes." He held the knife an inch in front of Switch's eyes. "You keep this blade in nice shape?"

He quivered.

"Huh?" the customer asked.

Switch responded with an erratic nod.

"Good, good." The customer fell silent and lowered his head into his chest. "Name's Warren," he muttered after moment.

He smashed the handle of the blade against his arm again, and said, "I mean, *Jesus*, why couldn't you guys—Why couldn't you just *fucking* listen—I'm sick —fucking eyes—seeing me before I made a move. What the fuck?" Warren tossed the knife back and forth between his hands.

Switch, unlike Lotus, remained seated and bounded by a heavy, greasy chain; Lotus was held by rope. He continued to convulse in place.

Warren rushed up to him and wedged the blade under the ball of Switch's eye.

Switch lost the ability to do anything more than sniffle.

Warren dug the blade deeper and deeper to keep the eye from crushing. The eye bounced like gelatin against the silver blade.

The eye slid out of the socket and rolled down the blade into Warren's free hand. He examined it closer and chuckled.

And Warren's smile faded. "Eat it," he mumbled.

Switch completely broke down.

"Now!"

Lotus couldn't force his eyes shut soon enough.

Switch lost control of himself when the acidic taste of the intraocular fluids caked his tongue. He cringed and bit down. His working eyelid flipped open as he felt the *pop* and *crunch* along his molars.

The sound of Switch retching on the damp concrete compelled Lotus to turn away and do the same. When his eyes reconnected with the grim sight in the corner, Warren began working out the next eye.

He pried it loose from the socket with the blood-soaked edge of the switchblade. A dry whimper escaped from Switch's throat. And even through the dim lighting, Lotus could tell the will to live no longer existed in his composure. He couldn't even scream. Perhaps, if given his options again, Switch would have chosen death.

As Lotus watched, the room blurred. His focus evaporated until he could see colorful speckles in the warm, still air.

VIV.

When Lotus awoke again, a single light hanging from exposed wires swayed. A whirlwind of dust spun overhead, and below sat Switch, shaken and quiet. His eyelids were stitched shut and bled from the corners.

Warren hid somewhere.

The only sound was that of Switch trying to regain himself.

"I'm sorry," Lotus whispered.

Switch didn't reply.

"I'm sorry all this happened. I should've never roped you into this life."

Still, Switch remained to himself.

"The hell of it is," Lotus continued, "I had a nice apartment and a nice girl—Melissa—but when she left, she took everything. Even my damn Chevy. And now look at us. Look what I've become. Look what I made you do."

Footsteps splashed water against the concrete.

The ripples sent a current for Lotus' feet, which carried over the switchblade. Something worried him about how obvious the knife looked, but as the footsteps drew nearer, Lotus teetered in his seat.

The footsteps drew louder.

His chair rocked on two legs. Then one.

And the footsteps were closer.

The chair tipped and Lotus' head smacked against the concrete. When he regained the strength, he used his forehead to bring the knife closer to him.

He pushed it into his hands, and the footsteps amplified, accompanied by the continuous splash of water. On his side, Lotus struggled to cut through the rope on his legs. As panic consumed him, he dropped the knife and worked his fingers between the knot, and within a few long seconds, freed his hands.

All that remained was the escape from the room. Though his legs were sore and ached from the rope, he hopped to his feet and hurried for the light peeking in from the staircase with a loud *sloshing*. He stopped and listened.

The room fell silent. Even Switch remained hushed. *Switch*. Lotus nearly forgot about him, but knew he couldn't leave him behind.

A strong arm hoisted Lotus off of his feet and slammed him against the wall between Switch and the staircase.

Underneath the scarce light, Warren's bloodshot eyes beamed a hole through Lotus' head. "You wouldn't just leave your friend behind, would you?" Warren asked.

Lotus stared at Switch. His bloody gaps for eyes stitched shut. How could he ever leave him to die? How much help would Switch be now that he couldn't see? Switch would die either way, Lotus presumed, but one of the options would bring him down too. "I . . ." Lotus whispered.

Warren pulled him closer and said, "You what?" and then forced him back against the damp wall. "You *what?*"

Lotus focused on the switchblade shimmering near the fallen chair.

Warren glanced back as well. "You want it?" He let go of Lotus and laughed as he smacked against the cold cement floor.

Lotus rose and sprinted for the knife.

Warren remained static, watching.

Just a few feet away: the switchblade.

The moment Lotus felt the handle on his fingertips, Switch screamed.

Lotus sensed movement against his back, turned around with the blade open, and stabbed.

And vomited.

Behind him stood Warren with Switch in front of him like a shield. Switch grasped the blade and fell to the floor.

Warren chuckled.

Thwack! Lotus snatched the chair and whipped Warren across the head. Legs broke apart and splinters floated along the water.

As Warren crashed against the floor, Switch yanked out his blade and slid it toward Lotus. His eyes rolled back, and then he was gone.

Knife clutched in his palm, Lotus ran.

X.

Outside, the cicadas hissed from the nearby woods. In front of a steaming sewer plate, Lotus stood with his right arm holding the door open. Looking around, he saw the faded street signs and metal bars securing closed shops and homes. Graffiti gallerias were ubiquitous, and many apartment rises displayed damp clothes drying over their railings. The park stretched out behind the buildings. He knew where he was.

Lotus felt at home, which terrified him.

He let the door close and turned around. Next to the building behind him, an old Chevy Nova sat on blocks.

"How?" he asked the night.

As the cicadas faded away like everything else in Raven's Crook, Lotus approached the apartment rise and ran his finger along the callbox labels.

"Conner, Cooper, Cromwell." *Cromwell, Melissa.* With a cautionary glance behind him, he smashed down the call button.

It buzzed for awhile, but no good came from it, so he pressed it again.

A tired, smoky voice came over the intercom. "Do you have any idea what time it is?"

"Melissa, hey it's me," Lotus spat out.

"Levi?" she asked. "No, no. Fuck off, *Lotus.*"

"Please, Melissa, we don't got a lotta time. I need you—"

"—Don't give me this shit. *I need you, I need you.*" She mocked him. "Just go. I don't need this shit right now; not from you."

Something creaked behind Lotus. He looked back and saw nothing.

"You don't understand," he said, "He's gonna—"

From behind, a gloved hand grabbed Lotus by the jaw and pulled him back.

Melissa continued over the speaker: "No, I do understand. You've hit bottom again, or you're drunk. Or you were caught stealing or some shit. Fuck you."

Warren swung Lotus into a collection of overfilled trashcans. Lotus retrieved the knife after a crash of aluminum.

Lotus struggled to rise to his feet. He held the switchblade in one hand and poked the air around him until Warren moved out of sight.

A crackle from the sky alarmed Lotus just before it started to rain. Thick drops of water bounced off of him and the blade as the streets steamed.

A fierce push sent Lotus face-first to the ground. Warren hovered above him with a twisted grin along his soaked face.

When he reached down for Lotus, a sharp, heated pain rose from his stomach.

Lotus yanked the blade out from Warren's stomach and rushed off into the distance.

Warren staggered behind him with one arm over his wound. He sniggered into the vast emptiness, and he pursued.

XI.

Lotus felt his feet slip out from underneath him, and he met the rain-glossed pavement with a loud *thunk*. The sound went unheard in the town; it was more of something he felt.

He wasted little time returning to his feet. Up ahead, the steam thickened and came close to masking the Lakeside Bridge. It was one of two ways from Raven's Crook to Lakeside; probably the least favorable, though the most convenient.

He hesitated to evaluate his predicament, Sure, Raven's Crook struck fear into many night travelers, but so many people had disappeared underneath the bridge, which seemed far worse to Lotus.

But I'm going over it, he thought. *Not under.*

Something scraped the pavement behind him.

Lotus jerked around to see Warren sneaking up on him. Before he appeared so strong and intimidating, but now he was weak again. His hand covered his stomach, and his movements were unsteady.

Despite his better judgment, Lotus sprinted onto the bridge. Two thousand feet more and he would be in a better town, where there would be police to help him. He knew the risks of speaking with the same authorities that would love to put him away, but a life in prison now sounded better than a premature death.

Halfway across the bridge, Lotus searched for Warren, although he never stopped running. He faced forward—

To meet Warren clutching him by the throat. Lotus rummaged his pockets and found the knife again.

Before he had the chance to flick it open, Warren smacked the blade out of Lotus' hand. They both watched as the knife dropped thirty feet down into the Chase Lake.

XII.

"You know what's going to happen," Warren said to Lotus, his voice low and raspy.

"I'm sorry," Lotus muttered. He whimpered.

"What's that?"

"C'mon, just let me go. It'll never happen again."

"You don't get it, do you?" Warren looked around and saw no one coming. He tightened his grip on Lotus' neck. "You guys thought you were tough shit." He rolled up his sleeve with his teeth to reveal the tally marks along the scar. "So did these guys."

Warren whipped Lotus' neck to the side. "But there's always someone better than you," he said at the *cracking* sound of Lotus' neck as it snapped. He watched Lotus' eyes roll back and then kicked him in the chest, sending him over the bridge and into the lake.

XIII.

Warren smiled at the sight of Lotus' body sprawled out like a cross as he splashed into the water.

He stepped away from the edge and sat down, cross-legged. He held the back of his head with both hands and shook for a moment before returning to his feet and covering his wound. Ahead: Lakeside. Warren was almost home.

He headed onward, dreaming of how wonderful a shower would feel after he drew another tally mark on his arm. At this point, he couldn't fathom the comfort of a mattress. He tried to picture his body sliding along silky sheets. He imagined the burning warmth . . .

Coming from the center of his chest as a long blade pierced his flesh and slid through his ribcage. A shadowy figure wiped the blood off of the knife along Warren's shirt as he dropped to the ground and faced the fog and steam above him.

The shadow ransacked Warren's belongings and vanished back behind the smoky curtain of a Raven's Crook night.

Sleep

I.

Quicker than a blink, an Audi soars down the main strip of downtown Long Brooke and crashes into the side of the Hyatt Hotel.

Glass dripping red scatters through the air and covers both lanes and the median as I step toward the wreckage. I hesitate before the body. On the median once glowing with flowers from around the world, the driver's body lies flat-out, arms twisted around the torso, knees bent inwards, and a steel rod running down from the dead man's skull and out of his back. All this seems like *her* work.

I brush past the man, only giving him a moment's glance, and reach the hood of the car, where smoke from the engine mixes with the gleam of traffic signals and streetlamps to create a cocaine-club perspective of the night. Underneath all the smoke, I find a metal speed limit sign. The car crashed at around ninety miles per hour; the sign reads forty-five. This is how *she* can still make me laugh. Written on the sign is MELISSA EVE MAKER.

Such signs aren't uncommon these days. There's nothing more people like to do than put their name on someone else's demise. Back when I thought I was the only person in this town who couldn't sleep, I used to see wannabe gangsters spray-painting their names and symbols underneath bridges, on the sides of banks and buses, all along trains. Some people used to even paint their names over the engravings on tombstones, which made me sick the first time.

But now I'm not alone. No one in this town sleeps, and to be perfectly honest, it's really starting to piss me off. As though gravity stops working, I spin around in a circle and take in everything I can see through the nightfall.

Along the sidewalks are trashcan fires. Every mile or so there's a murder. Storefronts are demolished. Police stations are broken down brick by brick. There's no justice left in the world except for a first-come-first-serve policy on everything. And, of course, all around me are the names of everyone who can't sleep in Long Brooke. One side of the downtown strip is blasted with the As, as in Alex and Ashley. The other end gets a little tricky with the Ys and the Zs.

In the near distance someone screams as though they've witnessed a child or loved one die, followed by the sound of someone else guffawing as though they've won the lottery. Ignoring the sounds, I head to the Audi, which continues to smoke heavily, and I peek inside. Just as I expect, a can of spray-paint wobbles on the floorboard.

I place the can on the ground next to the body and retrieve the speed limit sign. I place the sign on the contorted dead man and pick up the spray-paint. Enjoying the hissing sound of the can spraying over the screams of the night, I write my name on the man's body. FREDERICK ADAM HOPE.

II.

It's two weeks before this mess started. It's dark in the makeshift den of my studio apartment, where I hunker over a keyboard and stare my eyes dry at a flickering monitor. On the screen is a search engine for careers and jobs. One by one, I flash through the details. *Writer Wanted.* So far so good. *Five years experience in the field . . .* the catch-22. From CEO positions to fast-food management, all these jobs have requirements that no one can fulfill. There are plenty of jobs out there, but no one's qualified.

It's nearing four in the morning before I reach the end of the first listings. My forehead sweats grease and my fingers won't stop shaking. I sip out the bottom of a beer bottle and set it alongside its five counterparts. The new bottle knocks over the bottle behind it, and a trace stream of beer splatters over my bills. The fat LATE NOTICE stamp bleeds red along the paper, despite my manic attempts to dry it off.

I indulge in a relaxing breath and rub my head. My slight reflection on the monitor reveals my sweaty hands have pasted LATE NOTICE to my forehead.

Snatching a pack of cigarettes from within the desk, I storm out to the balcony, where the cold breeze of the night used to be the only thing that could appease my racing mind, but Melissa took that away too. The silk sheets tracing her perfect frame would always lift with a passing gust seeping in through the window, like slow wakes along a shoreline. Now when I breathe, I'm choking on her.

Nonetheless, I step outside and light my first cigarette of the night. The smoke twirls around my head, something I can appreciate until it reminds me of dancing. Reminds me of wind. Reminds me of her half-naked under the silk sheets. Damn her, I mutter to no one. I cough as I speak to the darkened, quiet world. The smoke tears at my throat.

No sooner than I have the urge to wheeze, a light turns on in an apartment across the street. Someone else is awake. I've never seen an apartment light on this early in the morning before. Maybe someone is off to an early workday, but I doubt it. All the early jobs have requirements that no one can meet. I hack my brains out with the sour of phlegm in each cough.

I continue to watch.

The shadow of a young woman appears on the curtains. In a quick rip, the curtains part, and the blur of a woman comes to view. She stands forward and never twitches, nor do I. We stare at each other, and something kinetic happens between us. Not kinetic like energy, but like nonverbal magic. The knowing glances. The suggestive stares. Something like that, only she's telling me to leave. It's a territorial gaze.

I'm beaming one back at her. This is my early morning. This is my quiet world. I'm the person who roams around when the rest of the world is still sleeping. This is my stress, my insomnia. Not hers.

She steps away from the window and closes the curtains. They do a little jig before laying flat. A dance, like the wind and the sheets over Melissa's perfect body.

I mutter, damn it, again and flick my cigarette butt over the balcony. This is a five-hundred-dollar fine in Long Brooke, but at this hour no one will notice. Although I'd rather be in bed asleep like someone normal, I enjoy these few moments in which I can tell society and its pressures to fuck off.

III.

It's one week closer to the car crash scenario along the downtown strip, and an empty bottle of Ambien bounces off of the desk. I chug a giant glass of water and swallow. On the edge of the bed, I sit up and wait. I try lying down. In the midst of all this, my fingers somehow find their way back to the keyboard and start clicking.

Multiple job listings pop up again, and after sifting through a thousand unpaid internships, I find the shorter, but still somewhat long, listing of jobs. Requirements, requirements, requirements. None of these recommendations mean anything until I notice all the repeat names of businesses. Their names match the sorry letters and voicemails on my desk and phone. Millions of workers but only a handful of companies.

Like clockwork, I step outside and feel the breeze. It dances around me, like the sheets swirled up and wrinkled around the shape of Melissa's body, but her perfect little self is nowhere to be found. To be honest, I noticed this back before the first Ambien, which is what led to the second, and third. Fourth. I light up a smoke.

Across from my apartment, the woman's light is on again, and once again she is staring. My attention is torn away from her the moment I spot a second light turning on in her apartment complex. Then a third from the apartment below it. There's a thin scent of gasoline in the air.

It runs along the woman across from me, who has her head jerked out of the window. She's looking at the other apartments just like me. Something about her curiosity reminds me of the way Melissa used to rubberneck over my shoulder to read the screen. She would say, "C'mon, it's late. Let's go to bed."

I'm sorry, I would mumble a thousand times. I just can't sleep until I know what the future brings.

"The future is tomorrow too," she would say.

I tell her there's no way to be sure. How can I know who I am unless I know what I do?

Melissa's voice drowns away to the sound of the apartment complex in front of mine exploding. This is now. This is real life. This is what it takes for life to be interesting again.

How I reach the street in a matter of seconds is beyond me, but when I'm standing on the road, I don't feel so fast. Already a fire engine rushes to the scene, preceded and followed by a few police cars.

An officer stands on my side of the road and watches the blaze as others begin to fight it.

What happened? I ask the officer.

He turns to me and shakes his head. He says, "Can't be sure, but if you don't live here, it would be a good time to leave."

I tell him I live across the street and that I am just a concerned citizen.

"And I think you're full of shit," he interrupts. "But if you must know, we're already suspecting arson."

The gasoline drift.

But he doesn't mention the fuel. Instead he says, "It's been a common theme lately. A lot of fires. A lot of cars blowing up."

Cars? I ask him.

"Yeah, shit's happening and we're not sure why. Everyone around this town just seems to be unnerved lately, and then there are the fires."

Unnerved, I ask, not that I lack the comprehension skills, but because the last time I checked, *unnerved* wasn't a synonym for car-bombed.

We both stare at the flames as they sway in the wind, growing larger. Swaying as in dancing. Dancing as the sheets on my empty bed. Empty bed as in Melissa leaving me while I'm staring at my saggy eyes in the bathroom mirror. The mirror as in the medicine cabinet, in which a bottle of pills no longer exists. No longer exists as in my love, my handgun, my sleeping pills, and my sanity.

IV.

One bedroom light at a time and soon the entire town is awake. Hours before the dead man soared out of the Audi, he was probably fighting to sleep and decided to go for a nice drive. In this new world, you cannot be caught relaxing.

I stumble along the streets for awhile and make out more street-side fires and wrecked cars. Something about all the destruction soothes me. It's like I'm no longer the only insane person in this town. It's that thought alone which brings me back to my depressed, insecure state. If I'm no longer the only insane person in Long Brooke, who does that make me? I can no longer slap my name on absurd behavior, the one thing I thought to be uniquely me.

Underfoot, something slides and presses on my arc. And in the dim light of all the fires, I see an empty prescription bottle. It doesn't surprise me at all to see whose name is on it.

Something sparks above me. A *shatter*, a quick flame, then a sudden blackness. Someone has blacked out the streetlamps.

Lost in the darkness, I stagger until I feel cold steel press against the side of my head, followed by a smooth feminine voice saying, "Come with me, asshole."

There's no guidance along my path except for the cold steel pushing and the ubiquitous trashcan fires. The sound of men and women screaming crosses the town every few seconds, and somewhere there's the sound of another explosion. The whisper of gunfire. The sweet aroma of gasoline and sulfur.

We keep walking on for miles, the woman with the gun and me. A quick push of the gun urges me to stop walking. The voice says, "Here we are."

With a sudden *whoosh* of fuel, a dumpster at the end of an alleyway lights up. Along the walls of the buildings are the names of streets. Main, Greenwich, Evergreen, Moler. I ask what they mean.

The woman steps forward and waves the gun for me to see. My gun. Melissa holding it.

Oh my god. That's what I say.

She replies, "What kind of gun is this?"

I tell her I dunno.

"Where do you get the bullets for this?"

I dunno.

"How do you not know?" her anger is sweet. It dances like the sheets. Everything about this woman is beautiful. Her short black hair, her steam-punk appearance, those sapphires in her head. I wonder how I could be made out of the very same human clay, and I feel cheated by God when I see her, as though He made me out of aftermarket parts.

"There was one bullet left in here," she says. "Obviously, you know how to get ammo."

I ask her when she started to appreciate guns.

"My pacifist days are over. Now where do I get the bullets?" she asks.

Since when did she start to like destructive behavior?

"While you were asleep," she says. "That's exactly what I'm doing. Bullets, where?"

I dunno, I tell her again. I've never bought them.

"Bullshit, Freddy, there was one still in the gun when I took it from your apartment."

And the pills, I mutter.

"And the pills. Fine, whatever. But seriously, we can't be on the streets like this with only one bullet."

I tell her I've only ever bought one.

She slaps me hard against the face. Red like fire. Fire like the red of my sheets. Caressing her naked body. And so on.

"You son of a bitch," she cries. "Do you realize what an asshole you are? How long have you had the gun?"

I purchased the gun while we were dating.

And she slaps me again. I'm starting to enjoy the affection.

V.

Melissa's never been one to smoke, but in light of our recent predicament, she steals one from my pack and lights up with me. To my surprise, she doesn't cough. I'm provoked to ask how long she's been smoking and remind her how she used to yell at me for smoking, but my face still hurts. The lingering essence of fuel scares me away from lighting mine for a moment, but as I think about it more, I say what the hell.

We're both smoking as we sit on plastic camping chairs, the kind meant for kids. Lucky for us, American obesity rates are through the roof, so now a chair once meant to hold an eight-year-old can easily support persons of our statures.

There's something romantic about this moment, although I'm not quite sure what. Maybe it's reminiscent of some 1950s French film, in which lovers puff away at their long, skinny cigarettes before that first kiss. It's somewhat illogical since the stale taste of tobacco isn't quite the ideal flavor of a lover's tongue. More relevant, though, is the fact I swore to hate the woman sitting next to me a few weeks ago.

She lets smoke dangle around her lips and asks, "What made you keep the gun around?"

I tell her she knows why there is only one bullet, and I flinch in expectation of another open palm. Instead, I feel no pain. Could it be she no longer loves me, or is she one of the few people who believes sympathy doesn't always derive from misery?

She says, "You're stupid, you know that right?"

I shrug.

"You have a degree and all the writing skills you could ever need to get any job. Hell, you could write jingles for a living if you wanted to. And you're damn witty. I saw your name painted around town."

And I saw hers, I tell her.

"Then why the hell are you so depressed all the time?"

I can't help it, I guess.

She stands up and stomps her cigarette out. She grabs me by the wrist, and I stomp out mine. Dragging me to the end of the alleyway, she opens a box next to the dumpster and shows me a red canister of gasoline.

Melissa says, "Look, just look at gasoline. Do you know what's wrong with it?"

I dunno.

"It's stale fuel. When you improperly store gasoline, oxygenation takes place. Vapors escape. Even the wrong temperature can cause gasoline to become virtually worthless."

I nod.

She points to black goo around the sides of the canister. "See, that gummy resin is the degradation of gasoline. There's a real art and craft just to keeping fuel stable."

She picks up some litter from the ground next and tells me to feel the first of two sheets of paper. She says, "You feel that smoothness to the paper? How it's thin and slick? This all has to do with the grains of the paper and how they are woven."

I feel the second sheet of paper before she even asks.

"And this one, you feel how it's thicker and coarse? It seems to have a texture going both ways, right? Its grains are interwoven which adds richness, texture, strength, and a new appearance to the paper. If the first sheet gets wet, it's ruined. If the second one is exposed to water, it can dry out and become tough like papyrus."

At the risk of being slapped hard against the face again, I ask her what her point is.

Her red face, and so on. She says, "God, you're dense sometimes."

I tell her that's why she loved me.

"*Love*," she replies. "As in *I still do*. But I couldn't sit around in your apartment every night, watching you kill yourself over thoughts of the future. All you became was a pill-poppin' alcoholic, crying that he couldn't get a job. And then I found the gun."

I want to tell her I'm sorry, but I listen instead. This might be an important life lesson.

She continues, "You're so goddamn melodramatic with the one bullet thing. Sure, it's nice knowing you have control of your own life, but why do you only see that through the image of death? Look around. There's so much more to life than what you're killing yourself for. There's so much art and beauty in everything."

Like the gasoline and the paper, I mutter to her.

A slap for my sarcasm.

She says, "I did all this for you."

Did what?

"All of this. The fires, the wrecks, the people running around. I did this all for you."

I explain, while I believe she is a powerful woman, she couldn't have changed the town in a matter of weeks. There's no way one person could shut down the entire town.

"You don't have to blow up a building to blow up a building," she says. "I watched you and learned. There's so many other people just like you. You can take a perfectly reasonable, intelligent person and get them to destroy themselves and everyone else around them. All you need is a little stress and plenty of fuel."

I joke that I should turn her in to the police.

"This is serious, Freddy. Your doubt is exactly what chased me away. I watched you and saw how down you always were. I saw a perfectly good person being ruined. Open your eyes, damn it. The chemical structure of gasoline. The texture of paper. It's all beautiful. If you're depressed, you're not paying attention."

VI.

Melissa and I sit around a small fire we've created next to the dumpster, after deciding we needed to lay low. From time to time, angry Long Brooke citizens pass by and grumble, but none of them make a move toward us. We are merely two an insignificant.

For the longest time, Melissa and I just sit and watch the flames sway back and forth. The details all come out to me, including the way the light stretches from orange to blue, and the way the flames never seem to move the same direction twice. This is beauty of something common yet lethal.

Melissa watches me watch the flames, when her head darts towards the end of the alley. Two men steal what little moonlight seeps in. Quick to my feet, I head for them, but Melissa remains seated on the ground.

In the men's hands are lead pipes, in a synchronized fashion, they bounce off of their palms. All I can think of is the pistol not too far behind me. Only one bullet, but one threatening man with a pipe is better than two.

The first man to come into my sight is more like a human edifice. He towers six inches above me, and one of his arms alone could cover my entire leg. The other man isn't a model threat, but he keeps his eyes narrow and low, as though possessed.

One at a time, the men step forward, slamming the pipes into their palms harder.

Thwack, thwack.

I glance back at the handgun.

They step closer.

I run back for the equalizer, when Melissa shouts, "Freddy, stop!"

Melissa joins my side in plain sight of the two strangers. The buffer one steps forward and embraces her; a kiss on each cheek.

I shout what the hell? Leave her alone.

The two men chuckle and shake their heads at each other. The first one says, "Leave her alone? Man, you must got us all wrong."

The second: "Yeah, Damien and I—I'm Jacob, by the way—are here to help Melissa."

Help? I ask. Help her with what?

This time Melissa smirks at the two men. "With the big plan," she says.

What the hell is the 'big plan?'

Damien slides his lead pipe into a makeshift holster on his belt. Jacob follows his lead, and then grabs Damien's hand, clasping it tight and stepping closer to me. Damien pushes away for a moment, something strangely graceful, and leans down to tell me, "This woman loves you, Freddy, and you're just bringing her down?"

Jacob steps in and says, "But we caught Little Miss right when she was ready to call it quits. She told us her big idea, and we were in. We couldn't just stand back after hearing all this was about love and relief."

Love and relief? I ask. I understand the first part.

"Not yet you don't," Melissa chimes in. "Tonight you'll understand. The whole town will get what it so desperately needs."

I would ask what the town needs, but I doubt she would answer. Instead, I ask her how soon. It's about to be morning.

"And it will be a magnificent morning," Damien says.

Gunfire shatters our conversation.

I dart after Melissa and drag her to the pavement for safety. Damien's up ahead swinging at everything in sight, hitting a few men in suits and masks, but taking down no one.

The only one who falls is Jacob. A sudden second series of gunfire brings him down to the ground, blood immediately rushing out underneath him.

Damien drops to his knees and lifts Jacob's head. Over his shoulders, I spot three men dashing forward.

I rush to him with my pistol tucked in my jeans, out of sight. With the lead pipe in hand, Damien rises to his feet and joins me in pursuit.

Another round blows through the edge of Damien's hand, and he plummets to the ground with a *boom*. The man next to the shooter holds another device. Something squarer than a gun.

I feel electricity rushing through my body, and as I convulse, everything becomes a blur. Melissa is dragged out of the alley and the same with Damien. I am last, being pulled in reverse. The alley tilts to the side, and the art of fire fades away.

VII.

Blackness ensues, but the sound of Melissa weeping brings me closer to consciousness. I only see in shadows, but my vision returns slowly. There is the outline of Melissa, static against something tall.

I would die to hold her hand and soothe her. I would die to go back and stop all of this from being my fault. The unfortunate part of life is that it's linear, and foreshadowing isn't as obvious in reality. Or maybe it's what we confuse for hindsight.

"I'm so sorry," she says, making me want to tell her it's all going to be okay. But then she repeats herself a little differently: "I'm so sorry, Damien. This wasn't supposed to become so serious."

I can't hear Damien reply. That or I don't notice.

The color of oak comes out. The shape of Melissa becomes flesh, as does Damien's. Both of them are tied to statues belonging to an endless collection around the walls of the room, all in honor of past mayors. The chains holding Damien down smack hard against the oak flooring.

Everything about this place is so eloquent, and I'm starting to develop a distaste for all things beautiful. It's when I see the far-reaching bookcases and posh decorations I realize I'm in the Capitol Building.

"I'm sorry," Melissa continues to whisper.

I tell her it's all going to be okay.

"Not until I get my hands on that son of bitch," Damien says.

Who? I ask him.

He slams his fists hard into the ground and says through clenched teeth, "Ludwig. Those had to be his men. Just look where we're tied up. I'll kill him for what he's done to Jacob and me."

I urge him not to murder anyone, but he shakes his head.

"You still misunderstand all of this. It's not to kill; it's to make a point. I'll beat Ludwig senseless, but I won't kill him. As for that man in the alley . . ."

A flash of blood spurting from the back of Ludwig's head comes to mind. But it's Ludwig's profile from all of the speeches and campaign ads. He's merely a bleeding caricature in my mind before he becomes real.

With three men around him, Mayor Ludwig enters the room. He has grey hair around his elfish ears, but the center of his head is bald and reflective. He's a pudgy man the height of a hotdog. The men around him, however, are uniformly threatening. They're all tall, all the byproduct of physical enhancers, and all carrying guns.

"This is some shit that's been developing," Ludwig says, his voice echoing the effects of long-term smoking.

"You really don't know what's going on here," Melissa mutters.

"I'm not visually impaired, *Melissa*," he says. "I see what's going on outside of my windows. People are rushing around and destroying Long Brooke. This town has become sleepless."

"That's not the plan," Damien hisses.

"Not the plan?" asks Ludwig. "Tell me then, what is the plan? Why are these people trashing this building? Why are they hissing at me? Tell me, *please*, how the hell the control of this town slipped away from me in a just a matter of weeks?"

Weeks? I ask, though no one responds to me.

"Things escalated," Melissa says.

"'Things escalated', huh? That's it?" Pushed out by anger, spittle slides along Ludwig's second chin's second chin.

"But it's beautiful," Damien says. "Look at all these people, overqualified, underemployed, unemployed, disregarded, stressed, and lonely. Weeks ago, these people were confused and angry. Do you even know what it feels like to have worked for so long and then realize you might not ever be of use? Have you ever doubted your future? Have you ever, *ever* felt irrelevant?"

Ludwig is listening, but he has nothing to say.

And I have no idea what's going on here.

"These people are running the streets and being active about their lives. They're not trying to seize control of the town or anything, but they're trying to make a point." Melissa repeats all this as though it breaks the mental fog, and what's more agitating is everyone else seems to understand the current situation except me. Again, I'm left behind—the one who finds an enigma within clarity.

"They're not, huh?" Ludwig asks. "Then why are they making a mockery out of our laws? Why is the state calling me and demanding that I take control of my people? You say they're making a point, and I would be thrilled to know what exactly their point is."

I add that some of them don't understand the point. Of course, I'm keeping myself in mind as I scroll along their faces.

"These people just need to rest. Relax," Melissa says, and suddenly, things start adding up.

"You know what?" Ludwig asks. "You might be right. You guys rest here, while I get the rest of the scum off of my streets." He faces his guards and motions for two of the three to protect the room.

As he wraps his hands around the door handle, Melissa adds, "You know this is all *your* fault."

Ludwig turns around and glares at her. All color leaves his face, and he clenches his teeth tight, grinding them together while he approaches her one slow step at a time. "Excuse me?" he asks.

"You blame me," she says, "but you know this is all your fault. *You* ruined this city and made success impossible."

Ludwig reaches back and unleashes a fierce series of slaps across her face. The last connects with her left eye.

Damien and I struggle underneath the chains and rope to no avail.

"Watch your mouth," Ludwig says.

He walks away again, but no sooner than he opens the door, Melissa blurts, "Long Brooke will eat you alive."

Ludwig waves his arms towards her, and all three guards rush to knock her out with the butts of their guns.

VIII.

Before anyone can lay another hand on Melissa, I rock in my seat, tumble to the ground, still strapped to the stool. It's enough of a distraction to stop the guards from attacking her.

"Isn't this cute," Guard One says, "tryin' to be the hero. Tell me, was she that good that she's worth taking a bullet in the balls for?"

I'm clenching my asshole, that's for sure. I am timid. I am angry. But I am also determined and strong and totally shit of out luck, until a loud *thunk* consumes the commotion.

Veins bulging from his neck, Damien drags a fallen statue in front of him. He uses the chains to grapple it, and with the scream of a warrior, hoists it at chest-level and dashes forward. This has to be impossible, but sometimes the impossible happens.

Guard One flees for the exit, but I spin at his legs, sweeping him to the floor. There, he's all wide-eyed as the statue of a former mayor meets with his legs.

Damien pulls back and snaps the chains. He roars with agony or as though he's trying to threaten prey, before he slides underneath gunfire to untie me.

I release Melissa.

Damien blocks the rounds with another statue. He takes out the second guard the same way as the first.

I spot Ludwig cowering a few feet from the exit, which inspires me. Along the sidewall, I meet Damien, who is already holding a statue above the third guard—the one from the alleyway.

Squatting down, I wrap my arms around the base of a statue, and it nearly rips out my spine. This shit ain't happening.

With little to defend myself with, I grab hold of a broken section of chain from the center of the room on my way to Ludwig. Damien rushes up to him.

They book out of the room, which leaves Melissa and me an exit to the streets. Melissa joins my side, and we pursue.

VIV.

Only fires light the way as Melissa and I cross over to downtown Long Brooke and fall further behind Damien and Ludwig. Although they run away, there are plenty more eyes deranged and glowing and slicing their way through the unforgiving shadows of the crowded streets. Many of them are alley inhabitants curious about the more threatening men in front of us. They carry guns and diamond-tough glowers. Their index fingers are impatient to pull back the triggers.

All the while I'm transfixed on around six gun barrels. I can do nothing but ask myself how I got here. Melissa and I. How *we* arrived at such a hostile moment. What did I miss? I focus on Melissa's worried scowl, and it all comes together—crystalline clarity.

Melissa shouts, "You fucker!" and she has my attention. This is long ago in memory, but only weeks prior in real-time.

The walls of our apartment shake against the ancient floor. Old lead paint chips explode around my desk, or maybe that part is exaggerated.

Her next few words are jagged thoughts no more articulate than a drunkard's garble. What captures me—after I realize she has nothing to say—is her silhouette along the lamplight. It dances like the red sheets in a passing draft.

The meager light outlines her body, and even her shadow is angry. A moment of nothingness passes before I turn around in my plastic desk chair to face her. I feel the heat of my monitor burning at the back of my neck, which is from leaving a career search engine running too long.

How I wish I had something to say as I look at my pill bottle, but it does not play wingman or console me.

Against my assumptions, Melissa's next few words aren't ferocious: "You're so focused on what people think you should do, you don't see what people are doing *to* you. You wouldn't even notice if the world washed away around you."

What? That's my reply, and it's sadly the best I've got.

Melissa stomps to the far end of the apartment and rips open the door, letting it slam behind her. I swear she returns. I know I feel the comfort of her

lying next to me, but in the morning, she and
everything she owns is gone.

∞

The chill of the night chokes us, as though a toxic
perfume. Those with the guns are those with the
power, and they press against us, when laughter breaks
the tension and shotguns are tossed right into our
arms. The guns are some model I've never seen
before. Then again, I'm the guy who bought a glock
because it was the only gun I knew anything about.
And the laughter, it belongs to Damien, who pulls a
barely conscious Mayor Ludwig by his collar.

We have no chance of survival. We never did. The
push towards debt, the lack of opportunities, the self-
doubt: It was always and still is the fist pressed against
the meek. We're not trying to thrive, but rather, we are
trying to survive.

Melissa and I raise our guns to match those of the
men in front of us. We aim. As both of us tease our
triggers, she leans in for one last kiss, and a different
kind of fire fills the night. And suddenly, things start
adding up.

The Glass Box

Day One

In groups of three and four or in hand-clasping couples, the workers of Long Brooke—those men and women in bland business suits—passed by.

Some of them stopped to stare on occasion. A mid-thirties brunette woman, one of the few loners, halted in front of the glass box and stared at its prisoner: Dennis Rowe. She cocked her head to the side and made her eyes sharper than a new-age razor.

Dennis leaned against the box and pressed his lips against the cool glass, feeling the moisture of his own breath running above the fleshy crevices. He only uttered one word—a name. "Laura."

She narrowed her eyes tighter and stepped forward. Though the wind muffled what little could be heard from Dennis, she recognized her own name in the shape of his lips. No sooner than he finished the second syllable of her name, Laura tossed her body against the side of the box and began pounding on it with her fist, though to him, the sound was nothing more than a light *tap*.

Unalarmed, Dennis watched her lips move—how her teeth tore at her bottom lip. The trickle of blood seeping from the center of her lip reminded him of the decorative trees swaying behind her as they lost their amber leaves one by one. Slumping his head against the glass, he tried to listen closer to what she was saying, but he couldn't hear a word. He couldn't even hear the sound of the wind against the glass. Inside of the glass confinement cell, he couldn't interact with the world anymore, not that he ever did. Despite of all this, he said, "I'm sorry."

Laura observed the muscles all along his face, particularly the *depressor anguli oris* on each side of his mouth and how they were laced with age. The stubble running halfway up his face no longer held a handsome essence; rather it simply looked like poor hygiene and filth. She shook her head and twisted her body forward to storm off for work.

∞

Dust danced in drunken circles above the yellow mirror light as Dennis brought a cheap plastic razor to his throat. The dust swept into his nostrils, and his sneeze caused the staggering blade to slip upward. One drop after another, the blood stacked on the center of his throat, static like water soon to freeze into an icicle.

A six-foot, pudgy security guard clothed in a dirty black uniform stepped into the washroom and yelled, "All right, time's up. Get the hell out of here."

Three more guards dressed exactly the same with similar statures entered the shower room and forced the prisoners out. Along with his cell neighbors, Dennis dropped what he was doing, half-shaven and bleeding, and headed back to his cell.

The barred doors slid closed behind him with a *clink*, and the guard said, "Now you two play nice and leave everyone else the hell alone."

Ignoring the guard, Dennis strolled over to the back of the cell, where a man in his thirties hunched over a cement slab the prisoners called a couch. His cell mate sanded down his ass on the couch and stared blankly out of the small barred window. Outside the birds chirped, but they never came into view.

Not even the goddamn birds provided entertainment, but the man kept on staring out at them. He muttered, "Sometimes you can hear the birds, but you can't never see them."

"Hi, I'm Dennis." He didn't know how to react, for during his stay in the prison, Dennis only worried about getting out and never spent time thinking about the birds or dealing with fellow inmates. He remembered how he ended up in the cell after his ex-wife decided he'd committed a serious offense.

Dennis remembered the judge slamming his gavel down on the thin, black wood and how he thought a court room would be much different with large desks and oak pews and a large jury stand. Anymore it was about efficiency; everything cheap and frail.

Before he could offer some sort of response to his cellmate, Dennis was asked by the guard, "What's he doing?"

Turning around to face the chubby guard, Dennis said, "I have no idea, sir."

The guard retrieved a handheld device from the side of his belt, about the size of a book, thin and glossy black. He ran his hand over the device, as though his fingers were *magical* wands, and motioned his index finger downward. The screen brightened over his face, and he said, "Neville, Peter. What the hell are you doing?"

"Sins are now crimes, sir," Peter mumbled. "Thinking is not yet a sin, so I have not yet committed a crime, sir."

To Dennis, the guard said, "You keep a good goddamn eye on him. I'm holding your ass accountable for his." The guard continued through the motions of his job, meandering along the aisles of prison cells, taking a digital inventory of everyone's behaviors inside of them.

With his head tucked into his shoulders, Peter kept an eye on the guard, and when he was out of sight, he turned to Dennis and said, "Damn, I hate this. Last time I was in prison, there was respect behind prison abuse."

Dennis turned to him and replied, "Oh yeah? When was the last time you were in here?"

"Oh, I'd say about five—six —years ago. The guards used to know you by name then, too. They would beat the shit out of you the minute you smarted off, but at least they remembered your goddamn name. Now it's just loss prevention."

"Loss prevention, huh?" Dennis pondered for a moment, taking in those two words he'd associated with retail work. Product in and product out. He asked, "You got a name?"

"Didn't you hear him?"

"Yeah, he said your name was Peter. I want to know if you have a real name, like something people call you."

"Like a nickname or some shit, huh? Well, they call me Petey, which isn't too much of a stretch, I don't think." They shared a silence for moment, trying to avoid the one question no one should have ever asked in prison. Instead of *that* question, Petey said, "It's shit being in here, man. You know that? All that world out there, moving on and moving forward—progress, progress, progress. Touch-screen became that stupid waving system. Waving system became Lect Sync. *Lect Sync*: What a stupid fucking name for something."

Dennis said, "It stands for Intellect Sync, an Intel design for thought-responsive computers."

"I know what *it* fucking stands for. I just can't stand *it*." Petey stood up and shook his head. Pointing towards the small window in their cell, he said, "Look outside. Stand on this couch and look outside."

Since it was Dennis' first time in a prison cell, he complied and stepped onto the cement slab. He stared out between the bars enclosed with wired glass and searched along his surroundings, which included a small muddy lawn with a basketball court, a sidewalk on the other side of the street from the prison, and multitudes of digital signs displaying "Eat Here Now" and similar phrases above LED-lit golden arches and glowing circus-stripped buckets of chicken.

Beyond them, hidden somewhere underneath the smog, came the gleam of traffic. New cars with sharp geometric shapes. Fuel stations supplying everything but gasoline. And the court further up.

"Do you even remember anything before all this shit?" Petey asked. "Look out there and tell me you aren't disgusted. Everything is all polished and new, except for the sky. Everything is quick and progressing, except for the way human beings treat each other, man. And we're in here watching the world burn itself down."

Dennis stepped down from the cement slab and said, "At least you don't have the glass box."

"Oh no, man, you didn't commit lust, did you?"

Dennis held his silence.

Laughing, Petey said, "Shit, man, shit. That's fucking perfect. See what I'm saying? It used to be enough to steal from someone, but now committing envy or gluttony is worse. State and religion all in one, man. There was a reason our forefathers stood against that brilliant fuckin' idea, man. Now it's fucking lust—"

Dennis didn't feel like acknowledging his historical inaccuracies. "—That's not why I'm in here," he blurted. He sat down on the cool steel bunk and lowered his head. "I didn't fuck or whatever with anyone."

"Then why the hell are you in here?" Petey asked —the one question no one should have ever asked another prisoner.

∞

It was only two years ago, and yet, the world was a vastly different place. Dennis and his wife strolled around the new Long Brooke Mall, a place not constructed in the old cookie-cutter fashion, but in a way much like a vending machine.

Each store had its little slot, and at the entrance of each store stood a teller above a sleek black table, who would take a thumb-sized credit card from each customer and estimate how much each person could spend within a store without going broke.

Dennis and his wife —her name was Laura, her name was Laura—handed over their credit cards, and the teller waved them over a tri-beam scanner. After a quick beep, the teller station lit up their faces in white, and on the table the store's sub-departments broke down into sections on a holographic map, highlighting theirs in blue.

The teller said to them, "All right, you're gonna want to stay in the blue section if you plan on buying multiple products. If you're just looking for one high-end product, then go down and take the floorlator and slide over to the silver section. You can spend up to six hundred dollars and still be within your spending zone."

Dennis and Laura were merely browsing for Christmas gift ideas. Retrieving their cards first, they stepped into the narrow store, where an escalator on the floor beamed blue and opened. The ground dropped down, and the stairs appeared.

With a careful step, they hopped onto the escalator and rode down into the lower level of the story, towards their predetermined shopping area. Dennis glanced at all of the clothes on the main floor before he and his wife descended, which contained triple-digit torn jeans, floorlator-ready Converse shoes, and dress shirts flaunting small abstract designs on the sleeves.

Down below, the blue section never saw a price over one hundred dollars. All the dress shirts were solid dull colors, like faded yellow and grey, and all of the jeans were straight-legged and mass-produced. A few clerks strolled by and ignored them. Apparently, customer service only came with the silver department and higher. Higher literally meant higher in the mall. Stack liked children's toy blocks, the retail stores contained levels: Mid-floor and up meant expensive; down the other. Dennis recalled commercials he watched as kid, such things as phone advertisements suggesting his cell phone should be traded in because of its obsolescing age of two years. Feeling like he was behind the rich definitely felt better than being below them.

"What do you think of these?" Laura asked, scooting a motorized cart in front of him that carried two grey dress shirts and two pairs of dull black dress pants. "Your father would like these, wouldn't he?"

"I didn't even notice you shopping," Dennis said to her. Rubbing his temples he continued, "Why don't we just go up to the silver section and get him one nice shirt?"

"You need to keep up, Dennis," she replied. "You keep letting things move faster than you and you're just gonna fall behind. Just look at the customers down below in the red section."

The red section. Dennis didn't possess the slightest idea what the red section meant, but he figured it had something to do with being poorer than the rest of the customers. Maybe there weren't even clerks down there. Maybe there weren't even restrooms; he didn't know. The more he thought about it, the less he cared, and the more his head hurt.

Beside him the wall lit with a white presence—an image of a beautiful blond woman appeared on a wall screen. The wall woman asked, "Got a headache? Take these: Advil Express. 'Faster relief for a faster world.'"

Two cerulean pills rolled out of a small slot on the wall Dennis failed to notice before. Hesitant at first, he scooted over to the wall and snatched the two pills and dropped them down his throat. Without water, their chalky coating rubbed against his throat and scratched like illegal cigarette smoke. The wall woman said, "You're account has been charged."

Laura turned to Dennis after hearing the wall announce the price of the medicine, when the entire store squawked and glowed red. Four security guards rushed into the store a moment before steel gates closed all of the customers in. The guards sprinted towards a man trying to hide inside of the restrooms. "Customer," a digital alarm voice said, "You have removed a product from our inventory without first checking out with the teller. Police will be here momentarily to arrest you for theft, envy, and gluttony.

Please return the stolen items and comply. Thank you. Have a nice day."

∞

Feet burning from sliding around on the floorlators all day, Dennis and Laura stumbled into their apartment flat and dropped their purchases next to a slide-out closet, which upon detecting the products with it motion-censor, opened up and swallowed their gifts whole. A broken, digital voice said, "Good purchases. I am storing them in the closet for now."

"Thank you," Laura said to the wall. She waited for a response, and when none came she said to Dennis, "I wish we had the newer model that actually talks to you."

A talking wall. "What's wrong with this one?" Dennis asked. "It talks."

"It talks *at* you," she said as she headed down the hallway to the master bedroom.

"Maybe Santa will get you one for next Christmas." Dennis waited for her to reply, but only heard the sound of his own voice bouncing off of their undecorated walls. *Talks at you,* he thought.

Then: "What the hell is this, Dennis?" From the end of the hallway, Dennis heard Laura repeat the same six words over and over, like one of the animated walls supplying over-the-counter drugs in the mall.

His ass barely grazing the couch, Dennis jumped back up and rushed down the hallway, where he met his flushed wife and a soaring new-age razor blade.

One benefit of technology, in this case, was that new razor blades lacked the blade aspect—simple press of a button and the device heated the hair off of your chin. Getting hit by one, however, would still sting; therefore, he ducked down before the razor burned the edge of the door frame.

Keeping his head shielded by his right hand, he glimpsed his wife waving his paper-thin computer monitor at him. "Who the fuck is this?!" she screamed.

The screen viewed a picture of a redheaded woman kissing Dennis—her name was Sarah, her name was Sarah. Dennis and this woman, who was not his wife, lay happily on a sandy beach without a single piece of technological waste, save the camera to take the picture. The woman, a few inches shorter than Dennis, smiled through their kiss and flashed yellow eyes with the intensity of starlight.

He recalled finding her eyes most intriguing, for starlight was a rare fine in a world washed down with light pollution twenty-four hours a day.

"Who the fuck is this, Dennis?!" Laura roared. She slammed the monitor against the bedpost and kicked at the fallen pieces of nano-fiber shrapnel. Only in anger did Dennis ever see such precision in his wife—kicking nano-fiber was like swinging a baseball bat at a particle of dust.

∞

By the end of Dennis' tale, the dust circling around the small window disappeared and then reappeared again with dusk. The two prisoners sat across from each other, Dennis on the bunk and Petey smoothening his ass along the cement couch.

"Damn," Petey said, "so she found out about your little mistress, huh?"

Dennis shook his head and replied, "You know the thing is I tried to correct my life. I started seeing Sarah. It wasn't too long that we had together, but I did start seeing her after the divorce. I didn't just use her."

"Oh no, man, she filed a divorce? Shit, man, that's how they got you."

"And that's why Sarah and I didn't last long. But like I was saying, I tried to stop my *jackassary*, you know? Tried turning my life around, with just Sarah, without looking at any other woman. I tried to stop fucking up. I finally learned my lesson, but that's not the point, is it?"

Petey contemplated the notion for a moment, perhaps considering the crime for which Dennis saw the glass box. "No, man," he said, "it's not about learning from your crimes. It's about the punis—"

"—Rowe, Dennis," the chubby guard said from outside of their cell, interrupting their night-long conversation, "I hope you managed to get some sleep during all your bitching. It's back to the glass box today."

"Fuck," Dennis muttered.

Petey turned around towards the small window and watched the dust twirl down to the concrete floor. He listened to the sound of birds squawking and pretended to be unaware of the guard outside of the cell.

Coming inside their cell to escort Dennis out to the public realm to serve his punishment, the guard asked, "Is your buddy okay?"

"Who?" Dennis asked.

With his free hand, the guard slid his hand-held device and waved his hands over the screen. Over, over. Down, down. Next page. "Ah-ha. Neville, Peter. Pay attention next time I speak, dammit! We don't want to move you to solitary, but we will."

Is the glass box not solitary confinement? Dennis wondered. He didn't dare ask the question, and instead he held out his arms and allowed the guard to tighten his handcuffs, which were secured with a secret combination of numbers on a small keypad in the center. The guard yanked Dennis by his wrists and pulled him along the prison to the outside world.

∞

Day Two

On the second day of being in his crystalline confinement, hardly anyone who knew Dennis stopped by to look at him. Everyone passed by on foot or by floorlator, disregarding Dennis and heading towards their glass office buildings or to the mall. Around noon, Dennis squatted next to a small slot on the back of the box, where his meals were slid in. However, no police officers dropped by with his lunch today.

Over and over, he slammed his head against the side of the box and rubbed his hands over his stomach, as if doing so would alert a passerby to feed him. The thump of his head against the glass ricocheted off of the six sides of the confinement cell and burned his ears, like a misplaced new-age razor blade.

At the end of his thumping, the sunlight faded in front of him. He jumped to his feet and met his blue eyes with the infinite abyss of starlight. Standing before him, her red hair much shorter than before, Sarah stared into the glass box.

Dennis turned his head away from her, unable to stand the sight of disappointment painted on her face in the form of a lopsided scowl.

The box shook.

Unable to hear the sound of what shook the box, Dennis turned back to face Sarah, who stood a foot back from the box and pounded at the glass.

Behind her were the usual decorative trees losing their leaves in favor of the upcoming winter. Thick clouds of smog rose from waste facilities in the distance and rolled towards him.

Sarah—her name was Sarah—continued hurling her fist into the glass, a large diamond ring on her right hand scraping against the walls. She continued knocking without ever once meeting Dennis in the eyes again. Her fist drew red, like the beads on Dennis' neck in the shower room the day before. All at once, she stopped knocking on the glass and toddled away.

Once she was gone, no one else bothered Dennis, although he wished they would. The only movement near him took place on the front pane of glass, where Sarah had slammed her ringed hand. A small crack developed along the center, slowly running up to the top of the cell.

He could hear the whip of the wind; the sound of chit-chat and natural clatter. The wind howling against the crack influenced Dennis to gaze up at the sky. Above him, storm clouds rolled in and did not hesitate to unleash the beginnings of a down pour. His eye caught a gem of rain as it slid along the glass and snuck into the box through the crack. He pressed his chest against it and felt the fabric of his thick orange shirt catch on the jagged edges.

Yanking his shirt out, Dennis stepped back and began to punch at the box. When the punching provided nothing more than a cramped hand and cut finger webbing, he took another step back and kicked at the crack, and then hurled his body against it. Full speed, he charged into the wall and the glass shattered around him, to be picked up by the increasing fierce winds.

The rain poured heavier overhead and he indulged in the chill of the water washing the blood away from his knucklebone. Before he could clean off his entire hand and go out into the world, he felt a sharp charge at the back of his neck and plummeted to the ground, chest-first.

With blurred vision, he saw two guards standing above him, one with a taser and the other with a sack lunch. The two men hoisted him upward and tossed him back into the cage. While the guard with the taser stormed off towards a van parked on the side of the street, the guard with the lunch shook his head and said, "Tisk, tisk."

The taser-carrying guard returned with a small glass panel that folded out into an entire wall, and with a device similar to a nail-gun, he heated the edges of the glass and sealed them back together. "That outta hold you," the guard said, although Dennis merely read his lips.

As they started to take off, the passive guard stepped to the back of the glass box and slid the sack lunch through the small slot. "I dunno what this is. Enjoy!" And he was off into the van with the other guard.

Dennis let his arms fall to his side and his face sag. This was only day two. The world fell silent outside of the box, and the day continued without the slightest ridicule from anyone else. Nothing. No attention whatsoever. Inside of the glass box, all Dennis could do was watch the birds avoid the rolling black clouds and think, for thinking was still not a crime.

The Passive & The Consequence

I.

Mist blurred Jordan's view of the county road ahead of him, but he could swear the motorcyclist carried a body bag on the back of his bike.

Perhaps not a body bag but something smaller, the black bag bounced underneath the numerous cords which strapped it down. The weight didn't cause the biker to wobble along the road or drift between lanes, but it was far too large for any sort of motorcycle accessory. At the risk of hydroplaning, Jordan pressed down the accelerator and caught up to the back of the bike.

Minute by minute, the rain fell faster and harder, until the hood of his car vanished in the brewing storm. As he drew closer to the bag he stared at so intently, the biker sped up, drifted away, and dropped off of the radar.

"What the hell?" Jordan muttered inside of his humid car. He let the notion fade, if not out of fear, but because he quite simply didn't have the time to care.

He drove onward and pulled into the parking lot of the laundry mat fifteen minutes away from his home. In Lovington, Chase County, distance was measured by time, and anything under an hour was considered nearby.

From his trunk, he withdrew an overstretched laundry bag and slid it along the pavement as he rushed for the door to evade the downpour.

Inside, a few locals sat around, reading, struggling with crossword puzzles, and carrying on with cell phone conversations as though they wanted to be heard. *Everyone has their problems*, Jordan thought.

He placed his bag to the side and rummaged through his jacket pockets for a roll of quarters. Roll in hand, he raised his head and made eye contact with a Sasquatch of a man he knew by the name of Little Ben, from whom he tossed his attention away but to no avail.

Little Ben walked over to Jordan—a slow walk for a man, but quick for his size—and said, "What's going on, neighbor? Figured in your fancy house you would have a good laundry and dryer."

"A *washer* and dryer you mean," Jordan said. "Don't have one yet. Just hoping here soon I can afford it, if not a new house all together."

"Ah hell's bells, son, then we won't be neighbors no more. Man, you're the best thing to ever move next to me. Beats the old neighbors. Perverts."

A husband and wife pressing their bodies against a window without blinds. The wife dominating from behind. Yeah, Jordan had already heard the stories.

To avoid it, he replied, "So what brings you here?"

Little Ben rolled his eyes and shook his head an odd, slanted way. He said, "Shit, stallion, it's a damn laundry mat. I'm not race dating or nothing."

"*Speed* dating."

"Same difference."

Jordan fussed with the roll of quarters as Little Ben's attention drifted to a teenage blond girl walking in through the doorway. Jordan knew what kind of conversation would ensue, so he put forth more energy than he needed into breaking the roll open.

In a waterfall of silver, the quarters tumbled to the floor with a loud *clank*. Jordan dropped down to one knee and placed one hand on the ground for balance. He hurried to collect his change, place it into the washer slots, do his laundry, and get the hell out. He saw his neighbor enough on a regular basis—or irregular for one not so inclined to have testosterone-driven conversations at two in the morning.

"Damn, stallion," Little Ben said, "see the monsters on that one? I mean large luggage for such a little vehicle."

"I think she could be your daughter," Jordan said as he collected the rest of his change. That is, all but one quarter that refused to leave its groove on the sticky floor. He considered letting it be and moving on with his day, but it didn't matter.

"Nah, man. I always pull out. Shit, you still like girls, right?" Little Ben said without expecting a yelp from Jordan as a response.

He glanced down to see his big black boots crushing the center of Jordan's hand. He yanked his leg away and said, "Shitfire! You all right, stallion? What're you doing down there?"

Perked on his toes, Jordan shook his hand in every direction, spilling the change he fought so hard to pick up. Rather than respond, he simply screamed.

Jordan grabbed his bag and let the change stay scattered along the floor. As he dashed for the exit and to his car, Little Ben shuffled around his remaining laundry and yelled, "I'll be with—Shit, I'd take you to the hospital. Man, I will be right there the moment this shit dries. Hell's bells, man."

With little time to spare on conversation, Jordan tossed his bag into his car and started the engine. Before his engine completely *clicked* and warmed up, he floored it back on the county road and headed for the hospital underneath of the day sky threatened by clouds the shade of dried blood.

His speedometer constantly on the rise, Jordan watched for any sign of police vehicles behind him. Maybe his speed would cost him the price of a fine, or they could possibly send him to the hospital quicker. Nevertheless, he carried on.

With only one functioning hand, he fought to keep his car in the center of his lane, and the pool of rain water collected atop of the decrepit pavement served as no aid to him. Rain or not, he needed to have his hand taken care of as soon as possible. He pressed harder onto the gas pedal.

He neglected to consider the consequences of such a high speed during the genesis of a storm. What worried him was a truck catching up to him, though he didn't recall seeing anyone else on the road that morning, save the biker before the laundry mat.

The truck, demon red, came within a few hundred feet of him before Jordan felt the wheel slip from underneath his working palm. More than that, he felt his wheels do the splits and send him soaring for the edge of the road.

Shackled by gravity, his car bolted off of the edge of the road, came down, and slid down the center of the woods. It bulldozed every small shrub and tree in its way until the car spun sideways to collide with the side of an aged oak tree. His teeth cracked against the wheel, his broken hand hit the side of his door, and the airbag whipped his head back against the seat. The taste of blood. The fear before blackness.

II.

When he awoke, Jordan thought his soul had left his body. In the cracked reflection of a broken side mirror, he saw a mangled body underneath the damp fall leaves, sliced into several pieces. He only came to realize the body wasn't his own when he spotted the blood running down his broken hand and felt the numbing pain from his mouth.

"Shit, stallion! Oh shit. Jordan. Jordan! Shit, shit, man. Are you okay? You down there?" From somewhere above came Little Ben's booming voice. "Do you still need a ride to the hospital?"

Did he ever, but the words didn't come from his mouth. With what little strength he retained, he forced himself through an opening in the windshield and crawled along the hill. He could already see the county road, which suggested he hadn't hydroplaned nearly as far as he thought. One long reach of his working limbs after another, he worked his way to the road; all along the way keeping an eye on the body next to his car against the oak tree.

Right before the road, and before Little Ben hustled down to pick him up, Jordan fumbled in his pockets for his phone and smashed his hand against the entire keypad. After a sharp beep of hesitation and confusion from the phone, a voice said, "9-1-1. What's your emergency?"

He tried to reply, but with his cracked teeth, he could only produce a groan. Then he saw the body again and knew what the police would think. The best he could, he said, "I'm sorry. Didn't mean to." He hung up.

Little Ben already reached Jordan and lifted him up by the armpits. "God Bless America, you can stand!" he said at the sight of Jordan regaining his balance. Little Ben stared down the hill. "What the hell —Shit, son, you need a hospital."

Again Jordan tried to speak but couldn't. Little Ben aided him to the truck and slammed the door shut. He hopped into the driver's seat and sped down the road. In the rearview mirror, Jordan spotted the biker from earlier and moaned. He had Little Ben's attention for a moment, but not long enough to point out the biker dressed in dark leather from head to toe.

Little Ben must've raced along the roads before, for he showed no lack of competence on the road, even with the lightning overhead and static water below.

Within thirty minutes of Little Ben shouting out his familiar phrases and Jordan mumbling in response, they reached the hospital.

Before he could process the moment, Jordan felt his body lift up from underneath him. Little Ben scooped him up and rushed him into the ER, shouting, "This son of a bitch needs a doctor!"

The shuffle of people. Scared nurses. Excited doctors.

And the police.

Two officers dressed down in the usual black garb strutted to the center of the waiting area and waved over the doctors surrounding Jordan. Though only a quiet television filled the room, Jordan still couldn't make out what they were saying, but something inside of him knew damn well.

"Right this way," a voice from behind him said.

Jordan turned around to face a tallish doctor, something right out of a hospital commercial. The white coat looked pasted to his body. He was fit. Dark hair. Bright blue eyes. The fakest smile anyone had ever seen.

"Excuse me?" Jordan wanted to say, though it sounded more like, "Coozie?"

The doctor held in a chuckle and said, "Dr. Kevin Neil. Let's see what we can do for you here tonight." *Do for you.* Like he worked in customer service rather than the emergency room.

A nurse slid behind Jordan and tapped on his shoulders to ease him down into a wheelchair. She, like the doctor, had the calendar look—maybe a few extra pounds, but stunning nonetheless. And she had Little Ben's full attention.

"Shitfire," he muttered. "I'd like to—"

"Sir!" one of the officers shouted across the room. "Right this way." He waved him toward the congregation forming in the waiting room.

Before Jordan could take in a good look, the doctor walked in front of him, and the nurse rushed him into a room, where the doctor first took a glance at his wrist.

Once the nurse left, he said, "I'm not sure where to begin. See, you don't appear that badly wounded. A few teeth gone, sure. And the wrist."

"Bwookitatta lawandair mat," Jordan garbled.

The doctor tried not to laugh again. "Why don't we begin with the arm and do a couple of scans? It won't be until tomorrow that we can find someone to help you with your mouth.. But we'd like to make sure your jaw isn't broken, or that you have any cracked ribs or anything like that. Okay?"

∞

Hours soared by. Most of the men and woman working on Jordan blurred as his vision faded in and out from painkillers. When he came into a fuller consciousness, he found his arm in a cast, held up by a sling. They wheeled him back into the waiting room, where the police and Little Ben were still waiting. Discussing. Knowing.

They waved for the doctor to come speak with them. He heard Dr. Kevin Neil say, "Sorry, I have to mind the halls. You understand the nature of the facility."

One of the police officers turned around, and soon the rest of them followed his lead toward Jordan. Their glossy black shoes *croaked* along the clean, white floor. Their stares infected the purity of the stale air.

The bigger of the two officers said, "Sir, would you mind speaking with us if you are able to do so?"

Jordan wanted to lie. His legs worked. He felt better, his arm was casted, but he still couldn't speak to save his ass. The officer did not perceive his nonsensical blabber as a "no."

"We're going to have to ask you a few questions back at the station, if you don't mind."

Little Ben stepped forward and said, "No offense, Hawaii 5-0, but my pal here just fucked the shit out of his ass back there in the woods."

"So he *was* in a wreck back there. Look, did either of you call us during the wreck?"

The frail cop with boyish looks stepped forward and said, "These days, with all the technology and gadgets, we can track phones. All cell phones are turning into GPS units."

"What he means to say" the fat cop said, "is you called us and then left the scene of an accident."

"Hold on, hold on, soldiers," Little Ben interrupted. "This guy here didn't run from no crime scene. He's hurt. He's all shaken like a dog with blue balls. He just wanted help."

"We found the body at the scene," the fat cop said sternly. "Right next to your car."

Little Ben's eyes grew wide, and his confident stance turned into a weak slouch. "Shitfire."

Something possessed Jordan from that moment on. He knew he had to think quick, and surely a million excuses bounced around in his stirred head, though he didn't know what to say. Without his front teeth, he sounded even more like the kind of guy that would hit and run. He thought about making a b-line for it, but how would that look?

All of the thoughts passed when he saw the biker, underneath rain, staring in through the front doors. "Oookider!" Jordan shouted, his working index finger pointed at the front door.

The boyish officer turned and glanced, but the fat one stayed facing Jordan. He said, "There's no one over there."

The fat one said, "Nice try."

And then the notion returned to Jordan. All in one fell swoop, he slipped his cast out of its sling and slammed it into the fat cop and then skinny one.

Nudging Little Ben along, he raced out of the hospital and pointed him toward the truck. "Gwo, gwo, gwo!"

They both hopped inside. Though reluctant at first, Little Ben started the engine and sped out of the parking lot with the biker out of sight, but the cops not too far behind.

III.

Rubber *screeched* and slipped from side to side along the soaked pavement as the truck pulled over. Little Ben stepped out of the car, and at sight of the police approaching, raised his hands in the air. "Jesus Christ," he screamed, "put me in the car or something. I don't wanna be no accomplice."

The skinny officer did as he asked, while the larger of the two sprinted into the woods after Jordan.

Jordan slid along the muddy path, down to where he wrecked earlier. To his surprise, his car remained, but the body was gone. The storm overhead devoured any light breaking through the depth of trees and shurbbery, but he was sure there was no sign of the body.   Perhaps this made sense. The police already investigated and cleaned up, but the footprints leading further down the trail suggested otherwise. Jordan pursued.

Globs of rain bounced along the tree limbs and knocked at his sore head. He kept losing traction, and at times he sank into the mud. But he kept racing.

With a cautious glance over his shoulder, Jordan saw the larger police officer closing in on him. He was sure fast considering his physical composition.

So Jordan ran harder until he spotted the biker again.

He stopped in his tracks, and so did the officer. Jordan turned back to say, "Believe me now?" when a bullet soared through the center of the officer's forehead. Blood blasted out from behind as he dropped limp to the ground and was buried underneath the rainfall.

From the top of the woods the other officer called, "What's going on down there? I'm coming down!"

Jordan froze, stuck in the middle of fear and his own persuasion. The biker took off down the hill in front of him, but Jordan couldn't decide what to do. Wait for the cop and risk the biker escaping? His passive behavior led to this very moment, hadn't it? Then again, chasing after someone who tried to ditch a body and shot a police officer didn't seem so reassuring, even without his injuries.

For the first time that day—hell, for the first time ever—Jordan decided to take affirmative action and raced after the biker.

From behind him, Jordan heard the sound of gunfire again at the same time as the boyish officer's yelp. Then a *click*—the sound of an empty gun.

The biker might have been unarmed now, but that didn't stop the fear contorting Jordan's gut. Timid, he moved in his good arm towards his ribs and spun around in the center of the woods, searching for the biker in all directions.

IV.

Rapid thumps against his back jolted Jordan awake. All this seemed so familiar.

He couldn't be sure he was awake this time, though, for when he opened his eyes, he only saw blackness. Shuffling around, he felt a strange plastic fabric surrounding him. It wasn't before long that he knew he was in a bag, being dragged along the ground. He didn't have to guess who pulled him along.

One last brush with the rough ground underneath him, Jordan stopped sliding along. He heard the growl of thunder outside of the bag, when the edge of a knife tore through the fabric and let the rain gather inside. He fussed around in the bag as someone else continued to tear it apart. Blue and purple streaks of lightning reflected off of the blade close enough to blind him. As the water inside began to rise, two enormous hands reached in and yanked Jordan out of the bag and onto the soggy ground.

Catching his breath, Jordan peered over the edge of the cliff. Though the storm cloaked it from further away, up close he could see a pit reaching far past each side of the cliff and descending into an endless abyss. Dirt slipped from underfoot, and he started to teeter along the edge of the cliff.

Little Ben reached over and pulled Jordan back to solid ground. "Damn, stallion," he said. "Be careful. What the hell is going—"

A quick *snap* and the biker dropped Little Ben to the ground. "Sorry, kid," the biker said, "but you just happened to be in the wrong place at the wrong time." He reached down and whipped Jordan forward, carrying him across the ground by his broken hand.

Jordan writhed in pain, but soon the pressure transformed into a soothing numbness. Nevertheless, he couldn't gain ground on the biker. He shoved his feet into the ground, hoping to sink into the mud, but where he was, near the edge of a cliff, there was only loose rock.

With his right arm, Jordan stretched back and snagged the bag. He tossed it over the biker's head, and brought him down to his level. Back to his feet, Jordan tackled the biker toward the edge of the cliff, and with a final shove, sent him plummeting for the bottom of a pit, cloaked by the stormy day.

Jordan dropped to his knees and tried to see the biker as he fell. He gasped and leaned back against his ankles. He waited to hear the sound of the biker hitting the bottom of the pit, but underneath the complaints of the ominous sky, the *thunk* could have been masked. With two officers down in the woods, a dead biker, and Little Ben somewhere near the edge of the cliff, Jordan's only thought was to run. First, he rummaged through his pockets for his cell phone. It was gone.

Glancing over the cliff, Jordan searched again for the biker. *My phone's probably in the bag, down there somewhere with him*, he thought. Unfortunately, he found the bag.

It soared overhead and landed on the side of the cliff.

Jordan sprinted back for the road. His feet slipped out from underneath him, and out of instinct, he placed his casted arm out in front of him as he slammed face-first into the mud and coarse rock.

Rough hands clasped his shoulders and tossed him back onto his feet.

His vision was cut off by the bag being pulled over his head. Before it covered him, Jordan heard, "Leave my neighbor alone!"

Wounded, Little Ben struggled to pull the bag off of Jordan, but before he could, the biker shoved Little Ben towards the edge of the cliff.

Still covered by the bag, Jordan rushed forward and pushed out with his broken arm. As the eye of the storm ceased all sound and glitz, he heard an echoing *thunk* somewhere from down below. He ripped the back off of his head and surveyed his surroundings, hoping he'd pushed the right man over the edge.

V.

Thump, thump, thump. Something metal slapped the inside of Jordan's new washer as he tried it out for the first time. He pressed the stop button and opened the lid to peer inside. Nothing but wet clothes stuck to the sides, with no sign of anything metal. No belts, no buttons, no loose change. Nothing.

Knock, knock, knock.

Jordan closed the lid and started the washer again. With slow steps, he approached his front door and opened it wide. Before him, hair soaked from a recent shower, Little Ben stood with a bag of laundry strapped over his shoulder. "Hey stallion," he greeted Jordan, "couldn't help but notice you had a laundry and dryer installed this morning." He displayed the bag in front of him.

"Washer and dryer—" Jordan stared at the bag in front of him. Long, black, and weathered. The top of the zipper was torn from the teeth.

"Hope you don't mind, neighbor. Laundry mat was costing me a fortune."

Shaken, Jordan stepped back and pointed at the black bag. He asked, "Where did you get that?"

Little Ben took a good look at his own bag. He studied it, deep observation apparent on his squinted eyes. He replied, "You know what, I dunno. It was in my yard one day, so I figured what the hell, and started lugging it around when I did laundry. Thing's huge. You all right, stallion?"

Jordan remained frozen. He couldn't come up with the words to convey the emotions or thoughts or whatever danced around in his mind. He felt sick. He felt weak. As his flesh went pale, and he felt he was about to collapse, a sudden roar brushed by outside. He heard the sound of a motorcycle engine stop.

No-Injury Policy

I.

Raphael Douglas Sr., the owner of the Douglas Lumber Mill of Raven's Crook, was a mean, old son of a bitch with a furious right hook.

Every splintered edge of jawbone grounded together like dry cogs underneath my face the second his fist recoiled. Underneath raxeira, he hunkered over me and said, "I appreciate your concern for your co-workers, but it's no good here. The reason we pay you is so it's not called slavery."

He thumbed close his coat and plopped into his mahogany and brown leather desk chair. From his top drawer, he pulled out an envelope and tossed it to my side as I fought to return to my feet. The cash spilled out against the nicotine-yellow linoleum.

He said, "Pick yourself up, Nick, and go home early. Work tomorrow as usual and not one goddamn word, you understand me?"

I nodded.

"Good. Now go. You fell on the job. There's a no-injury policy, so I sent you home early. All right?"

I nodded again. I could smell the build-up of blood in my nostrils. Money tucked into my pocket, I stumbled out of Mr. Douglas' office and never dared to look back.

II.

Several months before the incident, I stood before the Douglas Mill on a cold October morning with high hopes and a future pointed towards promise.

These were tough times for anyone back then, since Chase County peeked at an economic downturn during the big two wars. Although I wore a torn coat and holey dress pants, I could've been mistaken as one of the fortunate. At this point, I'd already heard the stories of cruelty, abuse, and poor work environment, but I couldn't have cared less.

∞

Underneath candlelight, Allison and I sat across from each other at our make-shift kitchen table. Though far too late for dinner, it was a relief after a long night with Elizabeth. To eat and unwind was good enough. Eating a meal was a godsend. Dinner tonight was tomato soup.

"Henry stopped by today in his automobile," Allison said between slurps of cold soup.

I mumbled, "How's he doing?"

"He said he can't wait too much longer, Nick."

"How much?"

Allison slid her soup to the side, an act I'd seen countless times. She won't eat for the sake of emphasis. "No longer. You need to get a job, Nick."

I might've cringed as I swallowed tomato soup, but maybe I hid it well. I finished my bowl and slammed it against the table. I could be empathic too. "You know what it's like for me."

"It's the same for everyone," she said. "Get a job." She crossed her arms and slid her chair back, ready to leave with the last word.

I stared at her soup and said, "Finish that, honey. We can't afford to waste."

With a defeated scowl, she dropped back into her chair and slowly spooned the soup into her mouth.

"Give me 'til Monday," I said. "I'll go to the Douglas Mill if that's what it'll take." I brought the bowl to the sink and added, "Clean these bowls before the soup sticks, will ya?" And then I left the room with the last word.

∞

Mr. Douglas didn't seem as cruel of a fella as his employees made him out to be. He offered me the seat in front of his desk and said, "I'll lay it out for you. It's $1,500 during the year, which is based on you lasting a year or more. There's a no-injury policy. We're not liable for your injuries or their compensation. These are tough times, Mr. Tanner, I hope you understand."

"It's the same for everyone," I said.

He shared a blank stare and remained silent for an entire minute. He finally replied, "Yes."

He slid me an envelope as a few technicians installed newer lights into his office. "These new lights are something, aren't they? They're supposed to last longer."

"Sure are," I said and tucked the envelope into my coat pocket.

III.

Three days before the incident was when the turmoil began. Elizabeth Joan uttered her first words after the technicians turned them on. "Pretty," she said.

At work, Kent, a guy I spent six days a week standing next to, came in with a face full of bandages. One around the top of his head might have as well held his entire skull together. From time to time it bled, so I asked what happened.

"I fell," he spat out. His words were angry, but his eyes, all sunken and low, were desperate.

The lunch hour bell summoned, which meant we had thirty minutes away from the machines. During lunch we sat outside around a decrepit picnic table, facing a giant fence around the mill. On a normal day, Kent would sit with us, but after he showed up with the bandages around his face, we never heard from him again. He hid all the time.

I turned to a tall fella named Matthew and asked what was going on.

He leaned in so close I could smell last night's whiskey in his breath. He kept his voice real low and said, "This ain't the first or the last of it." With a quick hand, he slipped a folded piece of paper into my pocket.

PREP ROOM 2 A.M. the paper read. Matthew said, "But this time we need to work together to find out."

∞

Allison was pissed off. In our bedroom as I changed, she said, "Why are you going back there?"

"A meeting," I mumbled as I tied my shoes.

"What kind of meeting?"

"A meeting. Jesus."

She gave me her *look* again, as in, "I'm not sleeping until you tell me." What she asked was, "Are you ever going to be home? Don't you want to see your daughter at least?"

"Look, you asked me to find a job," I told her. "I found it. Christ, Allison."

From the next room, Elizabeth Joan started to cry.

"Fine," she said. "I'll get it. Go. Go to your *meeting.*"

∞

Two A.M. sharp, I stepped into the preparation room of the mill, a place with lockers and work essentials before our shifts. Matthew and a couple other guys from the lumber line sat around a table. "Welcome," he greeted me.

"My wife's fairly angry about this," I said. "If we could do this as quick as we can . . ."

"No problem," Matthew replied. The others remained quiet. There were four of us in all. "Here's the slick and skinny: We're trying to get together a bunch of us guys to form a group."

"A group?" I asked. "For what?"

"You saw Kent," he said. "This has been going on for years; probably since these doors opened."

From the upstairs office, a light flickered on and then off. We fell quiet, but the silence was diluted by boots *crunching* against upswept splinters from the work day.

One of the men screamed.

A *thunk* came from nearby and another scream. Whether anyone followed my lead, I didn't know, but I sprinted for the entrance nonetheless. The only problem was, in the darkness, nothing stood out. No moonlight peered in through the windows (there weren't really any windows) and the indoor lighting fell short to the traditional because all the lights could be turned off at once.

I only saw one thing in the mill: the silver edge of a wrench coming down on me. Bracing myself for the blow, I ducked and thought of Elizabeth Joan .

Right before the wrench connected with my left temple, someone drove to block the blow.

I stumbled towards the exit, but dropped on my ass and watched.

Matthew waved me on, screaming, "Go, go, go!" but I didn't. The wrench came down on him god-knows-how-many times, tearing flesh straight out of his bleeding cheeks. Surely the man with the wrench was going to kill the man who saved me.

I sprinted over to the man with the wrench and shoved my shoulders into his abdomen. A loud *clink* came from the wrench against the cement floor, and as soon as he laid out flat, I picked Matthew up and rushed outside. What all happened, I didn't know, but my saving Matthew had little to do with bravery as it had more to do with the fact, after they killed him, they would have killed me.

IV.

In the small room next to ours, I held Elizabeth Joan for hours on in. This might've been the first time in months I'd spent more than ten minutes with her, and for what reason? Work paid the bills. It added the new indoor lighting to our house, but it didn't support a healthy relationship between my family and me.

While I held Elizabeth, all I could think about was what Matthew said once the mill fell into the distance. "Just because they pay us doesn't mean they can treat us like slaves. We are still human beings. We still have rights."

∞

I approached work with a bit of reluctance. I felt scared, and I felt violent.

All these feelings kept an ugly sensation burning inside of me. Outside, the air was a cool crisp, and people roamed around the streets to their jobs. If anyone painted the town of Raven's Crook, Chase County on this day, it would have been beautiful and peaceful. Underneath all the tranquility, though, there was so much noise.

Early, I spared a moment to step into the upstairs office, where Mr. Douglas sat in his chair and faced the door as though he awaited me. He waved at an empty seat in front his desk. The room held and eerie presence with the only light coming from the gaps between closed blinds. Around us technicians continued to install new lights in the office, until he waved them out. The door slammed shut behind them. Without so much as blinking, he turned to me and said, "You wanted to see me about something?"

How could he have known? *What* did he know? I replied, "Yes, sir. Some of us were worried—"

"—Like the men you were here with last night?"

"Excuse me, sir?" I could hear my body tremble in the chair.

"Let's get down to the point," he said as he slipped rings around his fingers, one at a time. "Business is business. That's the best way to run a company. It never changes."

He stood up from his chair and drilled a fist into my jawbone.

∞

When I returned home, I checked in on Elizabeth. In her crib, she lied quietly. *Motionless.* In the midst of silence, I only heard two things: The first was my heart thumping against my ribcage, longing to escape. The second was her breathing.

A light broke into the room, and a shadow loomed over us. At first, I pretended not to notice. I faked stillness, while I turned for the doorway, inch by inch.

In a hope to catch the intruder off-guard, I jerked forward.

Out from the shine of light from the hallway stood Allison at the door. She said, "Come back to bed. It's late."

Something paralyzed me, and for a moment, I remained static in the middle of the room.

"Come on," she said.

I listened. On our way to the bedroom, she stared at me for awhile before she said, "My god, Nicholas, what happened to your jaw?"

Against better judgment, I muttered, "I fell. At work."

Hours ticked by as we lay in bed. For mere minutes at a time, I joined Allison in slumber, but my mind kept racing. All I could think about was Mr. Douglas and what he did and said. Then my eyes drew heavier.

∞

A few hours before I would normally wake up for work, I heard the stairwell to the cellar *creak*. I tried to tell myself the sound came from dry wood *popping*, but the *creak* echoed through the entire house over and over. Soon it was followed by the *scuffing* of a shoe, and finally, a loud *thud*.

Turning to Allison, I saw her eyes were sealed tight, so I slipped out of bed and grabbed my M 1911, the best forty-five I'd ever known. I headed for the stairwell. When my footsteps traveled over the sound of the other's, the house dove into a depth of silence.

"Who's down there?" I called down to the cellar. Not too much remained down there, but the thing that still did was a big one: My safe.

My first step onto the stairs created another *creak*. Shaken, I stood at the top for a moment and gazed down. The safe, though it looked intact at first, at a second glance, had its door ajar.

"Who's there?" I asked again.

Elizabeth screamed in the distance. Soon Allison would surely awake.

I took another step down, still unable to distinguish the intruder's steps over my own.

A flush of heat brushed through the hairs on the back of my neck. I swung around, ready to fire, and saw Allison behind me. She jumped back and asked, "What the hell are you doing?"

"Just go," I said. "Take care of Elizabeth."

Once she left, after the little scare, my heart stopped throbbing and my nerves eased. I could hear the thick end of my breath.

Cutting through the darkness, the blood-stained edge of a clever soared through the darkened stairwell. Behind a serpent-like mask, the intruder came wielding a blade. And he missed. On his next try, though, the blade slid into my side.

I fell back on the hard steps and felt for the blade around my broken flesh. To my relief, the blade only grazed my side, and for the most part, simply stuck between my arm and my ribcage. I rushed to my feet and charged the intruder.

And then there was blackness.

Allison stood over me with one of her faces. She had a deck of cards' worth of those glares. "What are you, insane?" she asked. On the corner of her night gown, a yellow flower stood out of place. I assumed Elizabeth Joan did what I could not—showed Allison how she made us sick.

"Someone was in our house," I said with little energy to argue. My words were broken by erratic breaths.

"No one was here, Nick." Her eyes left anger to sink into sympathy or ridicule. "Oh, darling."

She learned forward to embrace, but I jerked away. Confusion bled across her face as her red hair glowed underneath the yellow lighting, and for a moment, I was left breathless at the perfect emulation of the devil.

Rather than waste time by saying more, I slid down the stairs and showed her the open safe. I pulled the door with my right hand, impatient to see my worst fears.

Allison gasped and said, "They stole everything!"

V.

Sunday, the day after the robbery, I broke into the Douglas Mill by kicking in a side door. A few feet away from the open door, I favored my ankle. The door had a steel frame.

"Douglas!" I called out into the vast emptiness. "I know that was you last night!"

Only darkness and silence answered me.

"Or your doing," I trailed on.

Up ahead, a yellow glow sprayed down the staircase to the main office. I pursued.

All of the lights in Douglas' office appeared to be finished, but when I flipped the switch, nothing happened. Out of the entire mill, his office was the most overshadowed.

"I know you're here," I said.

Still, no one responded.

Hands feeling my surroundings, I walked back to his desk. As well-to-do as Douglas pretended to be, his desk was rather tarnished. Around the edges wood splintered off; some of it pricked at my finger webbing. I stopped at the side drawers. None of them resisted opening. In the first drawer, I pulled out each item and held it up to the dim light seeping in from the staircase to the side of the window. Some cigars, stamps, envelopes, and a pistol.

"C'mon, you cheap bastard. Where's your—*my*—money?"

The second drawer contained a small safe. Inside, I knew I would find all my savings.

Along the top of his desk were pens of sorts, but nothing with which to pick a lock. Perhaps his supplies were in a good measure.

I opened the last drawer.

At the bottom, underneath paperwork and a box of some sort, was a set of keys—they must've belonged to every lock in the mill. One by one, I tried the keys out on the safe, and one by one, they failed.

Sometime around the sixth key, I heard the *creak* of leather from outside of the office.

A sliver of light pierced through the dark room as the door opened.

"I hear you," a voice hissed.

Creak. Creak.

"I felt you move."

Creak.

"I can smell you. Regret. Fear. It all leaves an odor."

Creak.

I hid beside what I assumed to be a bookshelf and waited for the footsteps to draw near. Nothing before in my life had ever rendered me so terrified and useless. When I wanted to strike the most, I had to wait.

Creak.

He said, "Where are you? You know you don't belong here."

All I could think about, as he neared me, was the handgun nested in the top drawer. This could've been over with one pull of the trigger, yet this man hadn't threatened me. I kept waiting.

Creak. Creak.

The sound must've been right in front of me, but I couldn't move. Fearing I'd harm an innocent man, I remained paralyzed. It didn't matter how I looked at it, fear froze my legs. A chilling hesitance coursed through my body bone by bone.

It stopped and I jolted to my feet with a hard side arm to the intruder. Or maybe *I* was the intruder.

Though I swear I felt his head *clack* against my elbow, when I stopped pushing forward, there was a certain nothingness around me. In a mere few seconds how could've he evaded me?

A sudden strike to the back of my neck— something steel, heavy. When the cool metal met my skin, the pressure and pain weren't so bad; I thought I could handle it. Turning around, my entire body ached and dissolved into the ground.

I possessed no strength at all. I possessed no strength until Elizabeth Joan flashed in my mind. I had to come out of this office alive.

VI.

Hissing. That was the best word to describe the man's breathing. He taunted in the pitch black office, his eyes glowing red. I had to escape, but he remained determined to keep me on my toes.

I slithered out from beside the bookcase and moved into the leg-well of the desk. Warm breath washed over my sweating, paling face. Wherever I moved, he stayed close behind. There was no escape.

He crouched down and stared into my eyes.

I prayed I'd remain safe in the shadows. Maybe I could see him, but he couldn't see me.

Through the blinding blanket, his eyes shimmered like a diamond under starlight. Sliding forward, he displayed his face. His eyes narrowed like a serpent's. His teeth were rusted.

He struck at me, both head and arms. I did all I could. I threw my feet out in front of me with no real strategy.

I attacked his fingers and head, smashing them with my boots. After a screech in the office, all of the lights turned on.

My sight represented static at first, though Mr. Douglas came through clear as he stood in the doorway. But the other man, he couldn't be found.

"Get up, Mr. Tanner. Nicholas. Get up," he said with a stern rasp. "What the hell are you doing here?" Then more calmly: "Is there something I can help you with?"

I rose to my knees; meanwhile Mr. Douglas eyed the open desk drawers. "You were stealing from me?"

My mind screamed no, yet I said, "You stole from me first."

Mr. Douglas chuckled and shook his head. "What in the hell are you talking about?" He traced the light switch with his finger and said, "You're fired," before turning off the lights.

VII.

Sunlight broke into our home through the living room windows, while Allison played with Elizabeth. Though decorated with homemade curtains too short to cover the windows and an uneven wooden floor with a couch sans one cushion, the living room made me feel truly at home.

Still, I felt unnerved even as I watched the ladies play. Both of them appeared so content with their lives. I always wondered what they did while I worked, and now I knew. The unfortunate part was, Allison kept glancing at the clock and then me. Without a word, Allison let Elizabeth Joan play on the couch. She asked me, "Do you have the day off or something?"

If I had told her the truth, she would have screamed. So I lied.

"I thought yesterday was your day off," she said.

Moments later, I would have continued the lie, and even at the moment I could have come up with something. I could have said, "No, I had to switch days." Instead, I said, "They let me go."

"What do you mean they *let* you go?" she asked. "Fired? You were fired?"

I nodded.

"You were fired? You were fired?!"

Elizabeth Joan began to cry.

I kept quiet.

Allison rose from the couch and slapped me red before she finished walking over. And when she finished, she slapped me again. "Why?"

I stood up and met her eye to eye, "Don't you remember he robbed us?"

"How do you know it was him?"

"Even if I tried to tell ya, you wouldn't understand."

"That's exactly it. That's. Exactly. It. About everything. You never, ever talk to me about anything. I don't ever know how you feel, what you're doing—"

I never struck a woman before, and I never struck someone so hard in my life. "Damn it, Allison. Damn it. This is all your goddamn fault, don't you see that?"

With a stern glare as sharp as broken glass, she ripped a hole into my forehead. Words—the right words—circulated and filtered in her distance stare. "What about Elizabeth?"

∞

Tuesday came around carrying rain drops that could dent someone's skull. Underneath the charcoal sky, I stood in front of the Douglas Mill and drew in a deep breath. Allison was right, that bitch. This was all about Elizabeth, not us.

Although I certainly didn't expect it, Mr. Douglas met me at the door and shook his liver-spotted head. He said, "It figures."

"I need my job back," I mumbled.

He waved me into the mill, on the way to his office. Along the walk, I noticed new faces at every lumber line. "You might've noticed, Mr. Tanner, that your friends are no long with us. Anyone in your little group has been ridded."

He noticed my blackened eye and bloodstained side. "Got you real good," he said. "Now, Mr. Tanner," he added as he opened his office door, "I need to know what kind of man is working for me. I need loyal men who understand the value of a hard-earned dollar. Mind you, I said hard-earned. If you can be that man, I'll take you back."

He pulled out an envelope and tossed it at me. I counted. Less than before. "I thought—"

"—Just take what you can get, Mr. Tanner. You do have that little girl to look after, don't you?"

VIII.

For the rest of the day, I stood at the lines and kept my eyes away from the other workers. I didn't want to mingle. I didn't want to gain their attention.

When lunch hour rolled around, though, I didn't have any of the machines to hide behind. Group by group, the men on lunch poured into the prep room and cluttered around the only table. I sat at the far edge and chewed on a sandwich. Though I fought to avoid it, my eyes darted around the room. I needed to make sure no talkers ruined my chance at providing Elizabeth a good life.

"Hey pal," some young kid, no older than twenty, said. "Ain't you the guy who got fired just awhile back?" He continued to nudge me until I couldn't stand much more.

I said, "Yeah, sure. I'd like to eat alone, if you don't mind."

"So are you still trying to create a union?" the young worker asked.

"A *what*?" I replied.

"Yeah, alotta guys out west are starting these worker groups for fair hours, rights, and pay. Their last fight was all the way back in 1866. This isn't new, but things have gotta change. No more eighty-hour weeks for chicken scratch."

"No, I'm having nothing to do with them."

The young worker slipped me a note and added, "If you change your mind, just follow this sheet."

The bell summoned, and I walked out of the break room, tossing the note in the trashcan on my way.

∞

Allison snuggled with both of our pillows when I returned home. I rolled around for hours, trying to find a comfortable position for my head. A few hours before I had to wake up, as my eyes dried, I saw something twitch.

Moonlight peered in and something moved again.

"Someone there?" I asked the empty room. Across the bed, between the posts, the reptilian face flashed back and forth. It appeared closer each time.

I rolled out of bed and paced around the room.

The shadows pounded on me, open hands coming from all directions. Nails tore each side of my face, and as blood poured from cheeks, the moonlight passed, and the face vanished.

VIV.

I knew the shadow still followed me.

The floor *creaked* underfoot on my way through the room.

"Everything fine, honey?" Allison mumbled, one side of her face smashed against the pillows.

"Yeah, fine," I said from the doorway. "Just going to get a glass of water."

"Oh good. Make sure you lock the door."

"What?"

"Your job. It's getting the best of you." Her eyes rolled back, and her eyelids closed.

Carrying on, I watched each step. Part of me expected to find the shadowy figure missing, while the other part suspected to find Mr. Douglas himself. When my eyes glimpsed Elizabeth's room, that's when I really started worrying.

Into the threatening blackness of the baby room, I carried on. No light from the moon or the stars peeked in. Only a strange light reflecting on Elizabeth's crib was to be seen, though the source of the light was not.

Elizabeth Joan slept, tucked in ever so tightly. I leaned down and smiled at her for the longest time. A cold hand wrapped around my neck and yanked me down to the floor, and blood trickled out from underneath a set of nails in my neck.

The struggle to escape didn't panic me; it was what happened when I pulled away. The hands broke down, brittle bone to dust and dried flesh torn apart.

"What the hell are you?" I said.

And, of course, the shadow disappeared.

Out of breath, I held onto the top of the crib and breathed in. With a sigh, I reached down to fix Elizabeth's blanket, but before I did, I checked around me. A cold chill crossed over the room, though all of the windows were closed.

Sharp talons ripped into the back of my neck again, a stinging hot pain leaving me weak. On my fall to the floor, my chin caught the edge of the crib. Then there was nothing at all.

∞

"Nick," a female voice repeated. The source sounded so distant, as though at the far end of a chamber. And again: "Nicholas."

Allison. She called for me, and I jerked upright on the floor. "What the hell are you doing, Nick?"

Elizabeth, despite Allison's mouth, still slept. I said to Allison, "You could ask how I am."

"I can see you're fine. What in God's name are you doing on the floor?"

I checked the back of my neck and my cheeks. The lacerations were gone. My chin was still sore, and therefore I knew, at the very least, something really happened before I wound up on the floor. "I don't know," I said. "I must've passed out."

"This damn job is driving you mad, isn't it?"

"That's why I tried to leave," I said.

"You really outta learn to deal with having a job," she argued. "I know you're so used to sitting around all day, but it's time to take care of things. I mean, we have a family now, Nick."

For a split second, I imagined popping her in the face. "Yeah, maybe," I said.

∞

Ferocious thunder echoed like a tree crashing onto the floor of a forest, or like a man after a three-aught-six blast. A sticky rain covered me from head to toe. Lovely weather for Raven's Crook, I thought.

I stepped inside and ran into the younger worker from the other day. He wore bandages all around the back of his arm and wrist. He wasted no time and said, "You squealed on us the other night, didn't you?"

"What?" I asked. I might've exaggerated my concern too far.

"Please, don't waste my time. You could've just said, 'Sorry, Alan, I'm not interested.' You didn't have to tell Douglas and his goons."

"Alan?"

"Yeah, asshole, that's *my* name," he said.

"Look, *Alan*, I didn't say a word. I've been there. I know what happens. I wouldn't even comment on the weather to Mr. Douglas. Man's a real snake."

"Uh-huh," Alan said. The shift bell rang. "We'll see about that later."

"What?"

"I said I'll see you later on." He walked away from me and soon started his machine in the mill. Alan was in charge of the saw mills, which were these four-foot tall saws on mechanical arms that would slice wood into boards within a seconds. As the saws wailed, I sighed and followed him in.

∞

Mr. Douglas roamed the floors for most of the day. None of us had ever witnessed him leave the office before his time to return home. Then again, none of us ever saw him leave for the day either. The way he ambled around drove us mad with curiosity.

His breaths sounded more like *hisses* as he passed by. He stopped at the saw lines as Alan screamed.

Tips of Alan's middle and index finger dropped to the ground, and blood covered the machine as it continued to roll over the back of his hand. The force of the blade shredding his hands pulled him down to the ground. With what little strength he had, he yanked back but without success. He continued to scream until his face ran pale.

I worked at a packaging line, but left my duties to help him out. Mr. Douglas stood at the side line, where workers were to remain, and watched me pull Alan by the shoulders.

I fell back as Alan came free. His scrapped body plopped against the cement in a pool of his own blood. I glanced back at Mr. Douglas, who ran his foot over a white line and said, "He was standing far too close."

X.

Lunch extended another thirty minutes for the saw line crew, while the rest of us watched a few men scrub the blood off of the floor. Some of the stains along the saw itself could not be removed. At one point, Mr. Douglas said, "Feel bad for whoever gets the red wood. We'll discount it at wholesale." And he chuckled.

Sometime around one A.M., Mr. Douglas told us to rest for tomorrow, an opportunity we all jumped on.

A flashing sky welcomed me outside. On a normal night, a few men would stand outside to smoke, but not tonight. Something was different, something unsettling. To my sides nothing stirred. I had every reason to feel paranoid after the saw incident, the vacant entry way, and the barren streets.

A loud *crash* came from the far edge of the property line.

A cat chased a few mice away from the dumpsters. I calmed down for a moment. "Damn," I muttered.

A strong fist cracked into the side of my neck and dropped me to the hard ground. A shard of glass tore at the side of my eye as I saw three men circle around me. All workers.

"You're responsible, you know," one of the men said as he clubbed me with an iron pipe.

I spat out a glob of blood and asked, "Responsible for what?"

The men took turns kicking me in the gut, while I struggled to rise to my feet. The man with the pipe said, "For Alan. You know Douglas tipped him over into the saw. All because you ratted us out."

Another fury of blasts to my abdomen left me near unconsciousness. I said, "I swear I didn't say a goddamn word, and are you sure Alan was pushed?"

"I saw it," the man said. He stepped in to full view—a real powerhouse with an impossible structure. "John. Just call me John. I saw him do something. He didn't push him, but he scared the shit out of him.

Like he slithered in front real quick and tripped Alan up."

The other two men pummeled me again until John urged them to stop.

I replied, "That actually makes more sense now."

John hoisted the pipe above his head, over my spine, and asked, "So what're *we* going to do about it?"

∞

Four A.M., the Douglas Mill dissolved into the depths of night and into utter silence. John and I led the other two men, back into the mill. I held onto my side during the walk, but with the group behind me, I didn't feel so vulnerable.

Light broke into the empty floor when we slid in through the side door. The office lights were off. We were good to commence our plan.

A smaller guy named Lucas placed a small bag on the ground and opened it. Inside were a sledge hammer, another iron pipe, and a wooden baseball bat. I grabbed the bat and asked, "What's first?"

Rather than respond, John stood facing the saw. His gaze analyzed the wheel, tooth by tooth, and he grimaced at the blood inside the saw's cogs.

Sparks flew around the saw line as we each switched turns swinging at the parts we figured to control it. We swung harder each time, and my bat broke over the teeth. Meanwhile, John unleashed on the control panel at the far end of the machine. His swings were rapid and unfocused, yet effective. Sweat dripped over his lips. Each strike with the pipe generated a louder *clank*.

I worried the noise would expose us to whomever might've lurked around the mill. Stepping forward to calm John down, I spotted a shadow peep out from the corner next to him. It rushed to his side.

The snake-like slits for eyes gleamed red for a moment. They seemed so close I could've ripped them out for myself. I dashed as hard as I could toward John.

"What the hell are you trying to do?" John asked. He stopped working on the saw line and surveyed the mill with me.

"I thought," I started to say, but I didn't know what I thought. Nothing unusual happened around us. No snake-faced shadow. Just us and our weapons.

And footsteps. They cluttered the silence and gained speed.

John waved his hand in the air, but no one stopped destroying the machines. He said, "Pay attention." He pointed at his left ear.

I lifted the broken bat close to my side. I listened. I whispered, "What now?"

John waved his arm downward. "Shh. Depends who it is."

"What do you mean 'who it is?'" Lucas asked a little too loudly.

"Shut up," the fourth member of our wrecking crew said.

Lucas lowered his voice and lifted his sledgehammer. "It's Douglas. You know it is."

The footsteps halted in front of us. A woman yelled, "Nicholas Tanner, where the hell are you?"

"Shut her hell up!" Lucas screamed. "She's gonna fuck this up."

John said, "You dumbass. She *is* that person."

I rushed to Allison. "Shh. Stay quiet. What are you doing here? Where's Elizabeth?"

Allison pinched me by my hair and lowered my ear down to her mouth. She said, "This is where you are so late? Fucking around with your little work buddies?" She took in all she could. "What are *you* doing here?"

Every light in the building flashed on and then off. John asked, "What the hell? What's going on, Nick?"

I said, "I haven't—"

"—Oh my god!" Allison pointed at a shadow swooping over John. It revealed saw-like teeth and drove them into his neck. Claws spun around and tore at his sides as smooth as the parts of the lumber mill. It tore and tore until stringed veins, muscle, and bone all snapped and ripped apart along with John's decapitated body.

The shadow tossed John's head at the back of the saw line, and the rest of the body crashed chest-first to the ground. The shadow moved out of sight, and the saws began to spin.

"Get the hell outta here!" the third member, Neil, said. He let his pipe fall to the ground and bolted for the side door, straight into the shadow's embrace with claws extending like elastic. It ripped into his neck, and he dropped like John.

Lucas, the fourth member, seeing his friends drop one-by-one, rushed for the prep room, and I pulled Allison near.

With her warmth against my chest, I slid over to a corner near the saw and hid. In another moment, I wondered why I didn't just save myself. Maybe part of me still loved her.

Lucas' scream dripped over the walls of the mill, and I knew I had to go down swinging. "Stay here," I told my wife. "Hey, Douglas!"

I waited in front of the saw for the shadow. I waited for Raphael Douglas, Sr. I waited to make a difference.

No one responded.

I continued a few feet from the saw and called Douglas out again.

Click by *clack*, footsteps once more destroyed the silence. Allison quivered in the corner, which told me someone neared us.

"Mr. Tanner," the shadow said. "I thought we had an agreement."

"Things changed," I said. I stepped forward to show no fear. "They got worse."

Allison shrieked. The shadow grabbed around her throat and held her near the saw.

"Worse, you say," the shadow hissed. "Maybe you need a better basis for comparison." The saw picked up speed.

The shadow ran a strand of Allison's long, red hair and made sure I noticed the blood run from her follicles as the saw ripped it from her scalp.

"Leave her out of this," I said through clenched teeth. "She has nothing to do with this."

"Then do tell me, Mr. Tanner, what your lovely wife is doing here?" Before I could reply, he added, "It's a rhetorical question, Nicholas."

Like a shift of wind through dust, the shadow vanished and then reappeared before Allison, to pull her to the saw by her feet. Her body fell limp, her head inches away from the fierce metal teeth, and I knew fear paralyzed her. My own body refused to move, but even as I gained the strength, some invisible force stepped between us, holding me back, as though I smacked against a wall.

"Let her go!" I cried out.

For a moment, there came an eerie nothingness. A sudden rush of chilling air, the shadow lifted Allison off of the ground and lowered her to the saw, inch by inch. I charged forward with the spiked bat.

After a *crunching* collision, all three of us fell flat. Grabbing Allison into my arms, I faced the shadow as it transformed into Mr. Douglas. He clutched a large opening in his chest with widened eyes as he dropped one last time to the ground.

Allison sat her head on my shoulder and sighed.

XI.

At home things were still. Frustration washed over me as soon as I stopped in Elizabeth Joan's room. Lying in her crib with a pillow grasped tight, she brought so much peace to my mind. Although Allison might've created the disaster at the lumber mill and left our daughter alone, I was glad she was still alive. "I love you, baby girl," I whispered to Elizabeth. "You know that, right?"

From downstairs, something shattered. Allison screamed, "No! How are you here? Stay away!"

I sprinted out of the room, to the front door. At the bottom of the steps, glass sprawled out everywhere around the entryway. Rain blew in the house with a violent whip of wind where the front door once was.

"Allison," I called out. "Allison?"

She lied on the kitchen floor unable to move and in tears.

"Oh my god," I said, "Are you all right? What happened?"

"No," she repeated. "I'm the distraction."

"What?"

Footsteps the volume of gunshots bellowed from Elizabeth 's room.

"Try to hold on," I told my wife. "I'll be right back, all right?"

Her glazed eyes looked at me as I started to head upstairs, and I could tell Allison was in too much shock to recognize the claw marks inches deep into her chest.

I would come back to her, I told myself. *I just need to take care of Elizabeth first.*

"Mr. Tanner," Douglas greeted me in Elizabeth 's room. He suspended her above his head as she cried and made faces to silence her, though she wouldn't laugh for him.

"You're dead," I muttered.

"Precisely, Mr. Tanner, which is why I'm here. And by the way, did you know your co-workers already received word about what you did tonight? How you ratted them out?"

"*You* told them it was me."

"You're so clever, Mr. Tanner," he said. He made faces to please Elizabeth again. "But if you were so clever, you wouldn't need to work for me, and you would know what's about to happen."

I said, "I'm done working for you."

"No you're not. Your safe is empty. Your wife is dead by now. You either don't have the choice or the courage to leave."

"Why are you here?"

"Like you said," Douglas told me, "I'm dead. But the Douglas name needs to go on. My son, you see, may not be the best suited for this curse. This power."

Douglas held Elizabeth Joan higher above his head and stared into her eyes. The red glow from the shadow came back, moments before the shadow peeled from his body.

I pushed as hard as I could go, but the shadow rushed into Elizabeth's body before I dropped Douglas to the ground and caught her in my arms. Douglas' body rotted away before my eyes: His teeth cracked apart like his flesh, and his bones turned to dust. When I looked down at the pride of my life,

Elizabeth Joan, she smiled back at me and giggled with a crimson glow around her.

Afterward

If you're reading this sentence, I thank you for reading the entire book.

To be honest, I'd like to thank all the readers who skipped this afterward too, but that's rather difficult to do without them . . . well, you get the idea.

But for those of you who have made it to this page, just know I plan on rewarding you. As a writer, there aren't too many ways that efficiently portray how thankful I am for you. You guys are the ones who took the stories off of the site and into the magazines like *Full of Crow Quartlery*, from the magazines to novels like *Excluded*, and now my short stories into one eerie collection.

Originally, I spent most of my time trying to figure out what I was going to say about *No-Injury Policy*. What could I say that I haven't said on the website? So instead of blabbing about how this short story collection came to be, I decided to spend the time coming up with a way to thank all of you. When it comes to how this short story collection came to life, the answer is simple: The readers.

And I think I've come up with a good way to say "thanks." Since I'm a storyteller, I figure another story might be in order—for those of you who actually read the afterward. This story is a little different than the rest in this collection. In fact, many have called it *humorous*. I'm not sure what it is, but I hope it entertains you.

Now for the bonus story . . .

And the Zombies Starved

Zombies were all the rage back then.

It started off with movies like *Shaun of the Dead* and *Zombieland*, all the comedic romance stories disguised by those flesh-eating beasts. Cara and I'd watched them all during their midnight releases. When it first began, I was just as much a fool as anyone else. That was true until I remembered my distaste for the film *Pearl Harbor*. Some said *Pearl Harbor* was a masterpiece in the way it isolated a personal story from something much larger. Critics said it humanized the United States involvement in WWII. I said it was populist bullshit designed to sell the same old Hollywood love-story. It was a multi-million-dollar rerun masked by something that looked like war in the background—a love triangle and explosions in the distance.

Such storylines could've been juxtaposed with any other set of circumstances: an interstellar dilemma, an ominous dreamscape on Elm Street, inside of a failing 50s diner. Back then, it was tongues in throats and, oh yeah, zombies eating brains. But it was all the rage and it had everyone hooked.

One night after work, Cara came home with an atrocious set of heels painted black and green with something I assumed to be a face of a brain-munching undead. "You like them?" she asked. "I don't think they make too many of them. They're Zombie Heels."

I nodded and kissed her before we went to bed.

The next morning, on my way to work, I saw dozens of women pass by wearing green, red, and purple variations of the same goddamn Zombie Heels. When did the undead become so colorful? Even at work, women wobbled in and out of the sandwich shop with the *click* and *clack* of cliché until I had my first apocalyptic impulse. That was, I wanted to shoot every last zombie-sporting sucker right through the skull. Zombies were never meant to be cute, colorful, or cuddly. They were—and always would be—a mixture of medical and social experiment gone awry. If Hollywood turned the stories of Jack the Ripper or Jack Kevorkian into whimsical love stories, would women start dropping their day jobs for the glorious life of prostitution or start carrying around their own IV tubes?

My only sense of relief derived from the fact, when the customers ordered their sandwiches, they asked for BLTs instead of brains. And I only discovered sleep when I realized that one day the fad would pass. Be it the end of my beloved creatures as they were in their raw, gruesome forms, but the end of mainstream madness nonetheless.

But it only metastasized. The following morning, I awoke to a *thump* on the nightstand next to our bed. My eyes peeled open like fresh blood oranges to see Cara hovering over me with a grin that slit her face in half. "Look," she shouted as she pointed at a book next the alarm clock.

I glanced over and saw a book with zombies on the cover. "Jesus, no," I muttered. I read the back cover:

Roman and Julia are forced apart by their wealthy parents, never to express their love for each other again . . . That is until a scientific experiment to turn their parents into super humans turns them into flesh-eating monsters!

"Doesn't it sound great?" Cara asked, truly impressed with her find.

"Do you realize what this is?" I asked her.

"Yeah, it's a gory zombie book."

"Gory—No, this is nothing more than Romeo and Juliet . . ."

Something boiled under my skin. Whatever it was, it hid under the façade of anger and consumed me in a matter of mere seconds. I snatched the book and showed Cara exactly what I thought of it by hurling all three hundred pages at her chest. The problem was, I aimed too high. The book smacked against her temple, and Cara dropped limp to the floor.

"Shit," I yelled.

Back then, the police were overzealous and overabundant, and they didn't care how or why your wife was unconscious in your bedroom. If you'd hurt her, the police would hurt you.

So I ran.

Past all the houses on our street, down through the shopping centers and glass testaments to mankind, I sprinted for nowhere. It didn't matter where I ended up so long as I was away. On my journey, though, something came over me.

Everywhere I turned there were watered-down zombies. Passersby wore tattered t-shirts with cartoon zombie prints. Chuck Taylors and high heels alike boasted some demented aspect of beauty coinciding with the zombie. Was I alone in the world? Maybe all these people were zombies in the Haiti sense; carrying on the last thing they were told or shown. On every corner, marquees contained zombie puns within the movie titles. There were zombies everywhere.

Enraged by the zombie rage, I hurried along my path of uncertainty, brushing by zombies on every crosswalk. I knocked down a woman in her forties when I saw her zombie earrings. I took out some punk on a zombie-themed skateboard and almost cried when I saw blood rushing onto the sidewalk from underneath his head. Right before I took a bus headed out of town, I knocked out all five members of a street band called The Lost Sombi.

Wiping off the sweat from my brow, I found a seat on the bus and tried to regulate my breaths. The bus reeked of cat-piss, cheap cologne, and mothballs. Together it stirred into a brew I'd associated with decay. Although my senses peaked and the bus ride was slow, I kept to myself. During the trip, however, I couldn't stop thinking about Cara. Did I knock her out, or did I actually kill her? How many zombies did I take out during my escape from town? It wasn't my fault—it was those stupid movies trying to cover-up tasteless and unmemorable plots with the walking dead. It was the devolution of mainstream society from Barbie to Zombie High.

Just when I thought I'd regained my composure, a little boy turned around and stared at me, before he shoved his Game Boy in my face.

He said, "I just got this."

While his mother tried to stop him from talking to a stranger, the boy kept yapping as a remake of *Zombies Ate My Neighbors* flashed on the screen. "See, you go around and shoot zombies with Super Soakers and kill them, and you can throw soda cans and twin-pops at them, and you . . ."

I punched the kid square in the face.

The mother screamed and swatted at me with a zombie purse, as I stood up and smashed her son's Game Boy on the grated floor. At once, the bus halted, and one-by-one, the travelers came at me.

Swiping the purse, I whacked and pushed everyone in sight until I reached the front of the bus.

Tossing the purse to the ground, I ran as fast as I could to an old hotel at the end of the next block. Inside, I pulled out all of my cash from my wallet and told the woman at the desk, "I need a room as high up as you've got."

She threw me a curious look and remained still for a moment. A phone resided next to her, a few inches from her anxious fingertips. She tapped along the countertop, her slight movements drawing more erratic by the second. The woman peered up at me, and I stared right back at her. As she started to reach for the phone, she pivoted around and grabbed the top left key from a pegboard behind her. "You'll need to write yourself in," she said before she slid a clipboard of forms in front of me.

Back then, time eluded me. I might've stayed in the room for a few days, although it felt like months. From time to time, I clicked on the television to see if I needed to find a new hideout, but there was one time when the evening news surprised me with a different sort of newscast.

On the screen, a woman so starved she might as well been a zombie reported the tale of a new cult hero.

A video package displayed dozens of people boasting hats, shirts, and lunchboxes with my face. Not only did the merchandise depict an unauthorized use of my character, but it placed a shotgun in my hand, pointed at a mob of poorly sketched zombies.

The videos of my fans cut short when the reporter pressed on her earpiece and said, "We're now going live to the hotel, where our 'cult hero' was last seen checking in. Breaking news, folks: I've just received word that police are now in search—"

I slammed my thumb on the power button of the TV remote controller and bolted for the window. The window wouldn't give as I tried to lift it open, so I grabbed the nearby end table and shattered through the glass no sooner than the police plowed through the door of my room.

Down below, reporters and a swarm of fans with my t-shirts all screamed up at me. There was a way out, for sure. I could've escaped through a set of emergency ladders around the hotel, but I hesitated at the sight of at least three hundred people cheering me on. Didn't they get it? I guessed there were a lot of people who didn't *get it* back then.

Now I had to choose between escape and perpetuating the very thing I detested. It was either that or I'd have to succumb to the officers' efforts to arrest me and go to prison as a wife-beater. One more glance at all the zombies below on the streets and I decided to do what was right. The right thing was not the rage back then. Arms straight out in front of me, I dropped to my knees and said to the police officers, "Please."

C.M. Humphries has a pen and a flippin' degree to battle against everyday norms and obstacles. If he can't afford to drive to the next opportunity, he'll run. If he can't run, he'll crawl. If he can't crawl, he'll dig his own grave and bring down the demons with him. If he survives, he'll tell the story.

He is also the author of *Excluded* and *No-Injury Policy*. His shorter works can be found on his site www.cmhumphries.com.

He has his B.A. in telecommunications from Ball State University (Muncie, IN) and currently resides in the hidden depths of Indiana. Along with his prose, he also blogs about many aspects of writing, the future, media, and the strange.

\

For more works, please visit

www.cmhumphries.com
facebook.com/noinjurypolicy
@1cmhumphries — twitter

Coming Soon to Follow "No-Injury Policy" . . .

Ashland's Asylum

a Chase County Novel in Stories
by C.M. Humphries.

www.ingramcontent.com/pod-product-compliance
Lightning Source LLC
Chambersburg PA
CBHW070748180626
46818CB00007B/3030